DEMANDS WITH MENACES

A Philip Bryce mystery

Peter Zander-Howell

Copyright © 2024 Peter Zander-Howell

All rights reserved.

Certain well-known historical persons are mentioned in this work. All other characters and events portrayed in this book are fictitious, and any similarity to real persons, alive or dead, is coincidental and not intended by the author. Real-world locations in this book may have been slightly altered.

No part of this book may be reproduced, or stored in a retrieval system, or transmitted in any form or by any means, electronic, mechanical, photocopying, recording, or otherwise, without the express permission of the publisher.

PREFACE

Philip Bryce is an unusual policeman. A Cambridge-educated barrister, he joined the Metropolitan Police in 1937 under Lord Trenchard's accelerated promotion scheme.

After distinguished army service in WW2, by 1949 he was Scotland Yard's youngest Detective Chief Inspector.

Bryce is something of a polymath, and has a number of outside interests – railways and cricket near the top of the list.

face.

"I wanted to talk to you about something to do with work, Vee, but I'm beginning to worry about you, my love. Is something the matter?"

"Not at all, darling. At least, not at all beyond the fact that I'm pregnant, Philip."

Bryce took two full seconds to absorb this news, and then almost threw his cup and saucer down onto the table as he jumped across the room to take his wife in his arms.

"How absolutely wonderful! No, my love, it's beyond wonderful – it's the best news you could possibly give me! But are you absolutely sure?" he asked, suddenly concerned again.

"Oh yes; I saw Doctor Fielding today. He's as certain as I am, and everything is progressing exactly as it should."

"So..." Bryce paused. He was experiencing some blurring in his eyes and realised he had a powerful need to swallow hard before asking, "...when is our bundle of joy due?"

"Around the end of April."

Bryce held his wife at a little distance. Grey eyes questioned large green eyes. "But Vee, why on earth didn't you tell me as soon as I walked in the door?"

"I wanted to darling, I absolutely did. But I've had a bit longer to think about everything. To be perfectly honest, Philip, I've begun to consider the reality of an infant in the house. It will be a tremendous upheaval for you – you have such a responsible and demanding job.

"Oh I know you've always said how you'd love a child of our own, and I know how well you get on with Alex's daughter, and with Angela's children. But when the crunch moment came, I thought you might think about the many problems instead, and change your mind!"

Bryce looked at her tenderly. "If you mean things like childhood illnesses and disturbed nights, or being unable to make an instant decision to go out in the evening – not to mention all the extra work for you when I'm away on a case – I've always mentally factored those in.

"More recently, when you became a business owner, I also thought about what adjustments we'd have to make to our household and lifestyle if a child came along.

"At all stages, you see, I've been thinking about this happy situation in a positive way. Darling, I'm over the moon! I'm just sorry that you've been worrying so unnecessarily – and all without telling me."

Veronica's eyes were also moist now. "I should have known you better, Philip, and I'm actually surprised at myself – and at my own reactions," she said. "But tell me, what changes to our lives have you been thinking about?"

Bryce hardly paused for breath as he enumerated the many possibilities he had considered whenever his thoughts had drifted,

CONTENTS

Title Page
Copyright
Preface
CHAPTER 1 — 1
CHAPTER 2 — 11
CHAPTER 3 — 21
CHAPTER 4 — 32
CHAPTER 5 — 45
CHAPTER 6 — 55
CHAPTER 7 — 65
CHAPTER 8 — 77
CHAPTER 9 — 89
CHAPTER 10 — 98
CHAPTER 11 — 111
CHAPTER 12 — 119
CHAPTER 13 — 133
CHAPTER 14 — 153

CHAPTER 15	168
CHAPTER 16	188
CHAPTER 17	200
CHAPTER 18	209
CHAPTER 19	216
CHAPTER 20	234
CHAPTER 21	248
CHAPTER 22	259
CHAPTER 23	271
CHAPTER 24	284
CHAPTER 25	296
CHAPTER 26	301
AFTERWORD	305
Books In This Series	307
Books By This Author	317

CHAPTER 1

Tuesday 31st October, 1950

"The Commissioner wants to see you tomorrow morning, Philip. Nine o'clock sharp. In his office."

"Very good, sir. May I know what it's about?"

"No. But he doesn't intend to sack you, if that makes you any happier," said Patrick Anderson-Hall, the Assistant Commissioner (Crime), smiling to himself as he put down the telephone.

Detective Chief Inspector Philip Bryce, at his desk in his third-floor office at Scotland Yard and finishing the last of his day's mound of paperwork, sat back in his chair. Although he had received personal praise from the Commissioner on three occasions over the telephone, and had spoken to him twice at briefing meetings, he had never set foot in the head man's office.

Concluding that only something very serious would prompt such an audience, but unable to think what it might be, he resolved to discuss it with his wife that evening, and put the summons out of his mind for the few remaining minutes of the afternoon.

**

Dinner in the Bryce household was the interlude in the couple's working day which they both anticipated with pleasure. Post-war rationing and shortages notwithstanding, Veronica was a capable cook, making the most of whatever was available to buy. Neither was fussy about their food, expecting only that it be edible before cooking and palatable after. When Bryce wasn't working away from home they always enjoyed their one relaxed meal of the day together.

That evening, however, Bryce noticed his wife seemed preoccupied, picking at the food on her plate, rather than clearing it with her customary good appetite. While not looking unhappy, and not exactly monosyllabic in her responses, she was not initiating any conversation in her usual way.

After dinner, Veronica poured coffee for her husband but not for herself. Instead of sitting beside him on the settee, preparatory to cuddling up together as they often did, she sat on the chaise longue opposite him, the low table with the coffee paraphernalia between them.

Bryce regarded his wife, poised and lovely, as she sat with her hands clasped in her lap. Veronica gazed back at him, a strange look on her as they often did, to being a father.

"Well, it's perhaps a bit early yet, but when you took on the business we engaged Dora to help in the house. At the moment she comes in three days a week, but we can ask if she'd be happy to do more. We could ask her for five days a week." He slapped his thigh. "No, hang it all, Vee; we'll ask Dora to do ten days a week – twenty if we need them!"

A laugh from Veronica at this light-hearted nonsense showed him she was finally relaxing, and he carried on explaining his more serious thoughts.

"What we'll need to talk through is how long you actually have to spend in the office, and how much you can do in the study here. We'll have to see about finding a nanny, although not necessarily a live-in, unless that's what you'd prefer.

"We can look for someone to prepare dinner for us and wash up afterwards; and someone to get the shopping and do the laundry. I'm sure the agency that fixed us up with Dora can find all these people and…"

Veronica's smile told Bryce that his wife was pleased with his rapid recital of 'mother's help' solutions, but it was the gentle kiss which she planted on his lips which finally stilled him.

"I think what I'm really trying to say, Vee," he said when they broke apart, "is that I don't want you to think of giving up your work. You're successful, and I believe it's very good for your brain, and your happiness, for you to continue. We can afford to find ways to ameliorate the minor difficulties that Junior Bryce will inevitably bring."

Veronica giggled. "We can't go on calling our bundle of joy 'Junior' for six months. We'll have to think of an affectionate holding name, a nickname, and it must be one that would do for a boy or girl."

"Absolutely. And before you ask, I shall be overjoyed whether we have a son or a daughter."

"I feel the same – but I have an unshakable conviction that it's a girl!" said Veronica.

Suddenly remembering that her husband also had something to tell her, she abruptly changed the subject. "What was the work matter you mentioned, Philip?"

Bryce found he didn't want to drag his mind away from the news that his wife had just given him, but he explained his telephone call. "I've never been told to attend the Commissioner's office before, so I suppose I ought to put on a better suit tomorrow, and look my sharpest. Actually, I'm not sure of the protocol – perhaps I should dust off my rarely-worn uniform.

"The AC wouldn't tell me what *el supremo* wants, and he must know because he said it isn't the sack."

"As if!" laughed Veronica.

"I really can't think what it might be about. I've not blotted my copybook in any way, so it can't be a hauling over the coals. Anyway, the Commissioner wouldn't get involved in a disciplinary matter. My only thought is that Sir Harold has some relative who's done that which he shouldn't, and he wants me to investigate discreetly and possibly hush things up a bit."

Even as he spoke, Bryce shook his head and squashed his first thought. "But, given that the old man has a reputation for absolute integrity and going by the book, that doesn't seem too likely, I must say. Added to which, I hope he knows enough about me by now to realise I'm completely the wrong man to supply with a broom and a carpet!"

"What about a promotion, Philip? Or a new post?"

"I think not. The Commissioner wouldn't normally deal with a promotion for someone of my comparatively lowly rank. And it isn't likely for another reason – I'm already one of the youngest chief inspectors in the Met." He pulled his wife more closely against him and kissed the top of her head. "And since I must have missed some obvious clues about your pregnancy, darling, I'm feeling like a pretty poor apology for a detective at the moment, and already over-promoted!"

"Perhaps the Commissioner has been asked to approach you about something else. A

Home Office secondment?" Veronica suggested.

This was quite plausible, but her husband was still doubtful. "There are one or two committees, I believe. But I'm sure they're for the most senior ranks – Commanders and Assistant Commissioners; hardly for middle-ranking officers like me. Ah well, I shall find out tomorrow."

The conversation reverted to pregnancy, babies, decoration of nurseries and all matters related. There were many important decisions to be made, but the happy couple spent much of their evening considering nicknames.

By bedtime, they had narrowed the field to one: Bundle.

***

At nine o'clock on Wednesday, Bryce arrived outside the Commissioner's door as arranged. Correctly assuming that this would only give access as far as an outer office, he tapped and went in.

Two secretaries were sitting at their desks. Standing by the window was a uniformed Inspector – a man whom Bryce couldn't remember seeing before. He was the first to greet the DCI with a polite "Good morning, sir."

One of the secretaries also greeted him, and pointed to a closed door saying, "Just knock and go straight in, Chief Inspector. Will you take coffee?"

Bryce accepted the offer with thanks, and followed the woman's instruction. Inside, he found the Commissioner and his own Assistant Commissioner, both in uniform, sitting on easy chairs in a corner of the large room. The two senior men rose to shake his hand.

"Take a seat, Bryce," invited the Yard's supreme commander. "We'll wait for our coffee to arrive before getting started. He settled himself in his armchair. "I've spoken to you about a few of your cases, and I hear about others. And of course I also read about some in the papers. In fact, I've even called for a couple of your reports in the past. Fascinating stuff."

"I'm pleased my reports are sometimes read, sir," said Bryce. "Since I give a brief oral report to the AC here, I'd always assumed that the written version disappears forever into a box in the basement!"

Both his superiors laughed.

"I've also noticed that in at least two of your murder cases of late, the victim was no great loss to society," said the Commissioner. "Doesn't that somewhat reduce the incentive to solve the crime?"

Bryce shook his head. "I don't find it so, sir. For me, it's as much a matter of professional pride as it is of justice. A crime has been committed, and it's my job to find out who is responsible. After that, others can decide what to do. Hartminster last year is a good case in point; the victim was a vile individual. I simply identified the killer, and left it to the local Chief Constable to decide whether to proceed. In the case of a capital sentence, it's for the Home Secretary to decide whether to recommend a reprieve."

The coffee arrived. Setting the tray down on a side table, the secretary poured three cups and placed them on the low table around which the three policemen sat. A jug and sugar bowl completed the delivery, and the woman unobtrusively withdrew.

CHAPTER 2

"To business, gentlemen," said the Commissioner when cream had been poured and sugar rejected. "Three things bring you here today, Bryce.

"First, we're pushing you up to Chief Superintendent, effective as of now."

Bryce stared at his ultimate boss in amazement. Yesterday evening he had roundly discounted the possibility of promotion, but today he found that Veronica's first suggestion was correct.

"I don't know what to say, sir!" he exclaimed. "Thank you, of course, but I can't quite believe this. I'm already one of the youngest DCIs in the Met, and one of the shortest-serving officers in my rank – and this is a double jump."

"We've considered all that, of course," said the Commissioner. "The fact is that your success rate has been quite exceptional, and your abilities are unquestioned. Anderson-Hall and I are entirely satisfied that there isn't an officer in the force who would think your promotion is undeserved.

"In any event, double-jump promotions are hardly without precedent; and never forget that people like me get to sit right at the top without passing through any of the subordinate police ranks at all!"

Bryce knew that this was perfectly true. Almost from the creation of the first police force, ex-army officers had been appointed to the most senior ranks, and the tradition remained. And this wasn't only in the Met – many of the chief constables across the country had no policing experience prior to their appointment. Bryce didn't think the analogy quite matched the situation at his level, but he said nothing.

The Commissioner drank some of his coffee. "And don't think we're doing this simply in order to deter you from considering a return to the bar," he said as he replaced his cup in its saucer.

Seeing the fresh look of astonishment on Bryce's face, the Yard's supreme commander smiled broadly. "Oh yes, I heard that a certain set of chambers was wooing you not so long ago!"

"Then you probably also know I turned them down, sir," said Bryce. "And regardless of this promotion, I can't see that I'd ever change my mind – even assuming another offer arrived."

"Fair enough, but your promotion is purely based on merit. Be in no doubt about that," said Anderson-Hall, thoroughly delighted that his protégé was fulfilling his prediction of rapidly rising through the ranks.

"Let's move on to the second matter," said the Commissioner. Over the next two months, several senior officers will retire. We're losing a commander, a chief super, a super, and a chief inspector – and that's just here at the Yard. An extraordinary exodus in a short period.

"I've been considering rearranging the structure of the Force, and not just in CID. My deputy has done a lot of the spadework and it's unfortunate he can't be here this morning to explain it to you. But I can tell you that he's a hundred percent with me on the benefits the reorganisation will bring. I've also had some discussions with the Home Secretary, so we're going ahead. An experiment really, at this stage, and if it doesn't work we'll have to reconsider."

The Commissioner drank some more coffee and continued. "You're heading up a new department, Bryce. You'll be responsible for dealing with requests from provincial forces and Metropolitan divisions, for help in the most serious or difficult cases. Obviously, you won't be able to tackle every case yourself, but we don't want you to lose your expertise by chaining you to a desk. So there's no objection to your getting out and about a bit, and keeping your hand in. I know I can trust you to see that the administration work continues efficiently if you yourself are away.

"You'll report direct to the AC here, but we're all very clear that you'll have considerable autonomy. A budget has been worked out, mostly for staff, of course, and you'll soon see how many officers of various ranks you can afford. You two will discuss that in detail, but in principle you can appoint who you like. I want your team to be the very best it's possible to put together. Comments?"

"What can I say, sir? This is the opportunity of a lifetime. Thank you again!"

"Good. Now, we come to the third matter. The reorganisation doesn't need to happen for several more weeks – when the first retirements take place. But something came to our attention yesterday which caused me to bring things forward.

"We have a new case, and the AC and I both feel that the people involved are of such prominence they will expect a very senior officer to handle things. No bones about it, Bryce, someone with your intellect is essential, and your social status is also desirable.

"So, your promotion has come earlier than planned." The Commissioner picked up his coffee cup again and nodded at Anderson-Hall to take over.

"Yesterday, the Commissioner received three separate telephone calls. The fact that these calls actually reached this office shows the position and influence of those involved. Not one of the gatekeepers felt they could resist the pressure to pass each call straight through to the Commissioner rather than transfer them to CID.

"The Commissioner has spoken to all three of the men who called. At this stage none has been told about the others. Each reported much the same story. They all received a blackmail letter yesterday afternoon."

The Commissioner intervened. "A few minutes ago, one of those letters arrived here by courier, sent on by the recipient. But during my telephone conversations I made notes of what all the letters say. No question that all three are identical in style and from the same author." He nodded to the AC to carry on.

"Yes, the style is identical, but the allegations are all different – as is the size of the respective demands. You'll see the detail later.

"The letters appear to be the work of an educated person. The two men who received the letters we haven't seen made a point – quite independently – of telling the Commissioner that the spelling, grammar, and punctuation are precise; with forms of address, salutations and titles all correct. That's also true for the letter we hold.

"All were posted in London, and all at the same time. They were collected from a box in Arnos Grove at seven o'clock yesterday morning. You'll need to check the previous collection time, but it would almost certainly be around five or six o'clock on Monday evening. So at this time of the year the letters would probably have been posted in darkness.

"They were all to London addresses, and were delivered within hours of the box being cleared.

"As for names, we have David Poole, the cabinet minister; generally reckoned to be a future Foreign Secretary and perhaps even Prime Minister.

"Caspar Charrington, Bishop of Crewe. One of the Lords Spiritual, and strongly tipped to move from Prelate to Primate.

Finally, Lord Hartley. Peregrine Hartley as was, before his barony for services to industry. One of the richest men in Britain, of course."

"You can see the potential problems, Bryce," said the Commissioner. "These are powerful and well-connected people, each notable in his own sphere. If this matter isn't resolved fairly quickly, there's going to be an almighty stink." He stood up and extended his hand. "Anyway, we're relying on you. Go along with the AC now, and familiarise yourself with it all."

The Yard's newest DCS and the AC shook hands with their superior, and turned to leave.

"Oh, and by the way, Bryce," the Commissioner called after them. "From now on, all three men must deal only with you. I won't accept further telephone calls or any other approaches."

Bryce accompanied the AC to his own office. This was another fine room, and not much smaller than the one they had just left.

"Who was the Inspector waiting in the Commissioner's outer office just now, sir?" asked Bryce as he took a seat. "I didn't recognise him, but he seemed to know me."

"You're known throughout the Force, Philip," laughed Anderson-Hall. "That was James Kitchen from Clapham. He's being awarded the George Medal, and the Commissioner wanted to commend him personally as well."

"The chap who jumped into the Thames and pulled out the toddler?"

"That's the one. A first-class swimmer, of course, but an astonishingly courageous thing to do at any time, particularly given the river conditions at the point he dived in."

Bryce couldn't have agreed more. He had read the newspaper report of Kitchen's action, and he knew the location on the river and its treacherous characteristics. Not for the first time it struck him that the reputation of the police, up and down the country, was quite regularly enhanced by the personal talents and knowledge which its policemen and women brought with them when they joined the Force, which often went beyond anything their formal police training could provide.

Anderson-Hall drew out two folders from the stack on his desk, and turned the conversation to the matters in hand.

"A few initial points about what we've been discussing. "First, Sergeant Haig. You've recommended him for promotion, Well, you've got your way. He's made up to DI, also as of today. You can tell him yourself, and he'll get a written letter of appointment tomorrow. As will you.

"I imagine that you'll want to keep Haig to help clear up this blackmail business and, in case you were wondering, it's quite all right for a chief super to have a DI as bagman. I also assume that you'll want to retain him in your new department.

"On that point, here's a brief outline of what we want you to set up," The AC handed over the top folder.

"Look through it all when you have time. Some of the people you've been working with will probably just slot in; but let me know if you want to get rid of anyone. You can also, within reason, bring someone else in from another division or even another Force.

"Your number two will be a critical appointment. It's up to you, but I think you should choose someone with a flair for administration – not just a good detective. I'll back you if you want to promote an existing Inspector to Chief, rather than use one of the current DCIs. There will be a few other promotions effectively within your gift; for example, you might want to promote one or two constables to sergeant.

"Let me know your proposals within a week. As for an office, when Tommy Burrell retires next month you can have his room. In a sense you're his replacement, albeit with different responsibilities.

"Now to your investigation; everything the Commissioner and I know is in here." The AC pushed the second folder across the table to Bryce. "This is the letter and envelope that have just been delivered by special messenger. They haven't been dusted for prints, but the Chief was meticulous about not touching them. Chances of our blackmailer leaving his greasy dabs on anything must be nil, but you'll have to check.

"Blackmail is a dirty business. Take all that away with you and do the best you can with it, as quickly as you can; and don't think the Commissioner and I underestimate the challenges this particular case presents.

"The three Westminster grandees have been told that you'll be in contact today. I leave it to you as to whether to tell each one of the existence of the others. That's about the size of it, Philip."

Anderson-Hall stood up and offered his hand with a smile.

"Just one thing before I go, sir, said Bryce. "Veronica and I are expecting a child – due at the end of April."

The AC, who had known Veronica for some years before she met her husband, was genuinely delighted. "Oh, that's marvellous news! Congratulations to you both, and give my very best wishes to your lovely wife. I suppose I'd better start looking in silverware shops for a tankard or something. I don't even know what would be appropriate if it's a girl – I'll have to take advice on that point!"

"That would be appreciated, sir, of course," said Bryce. "But we both owe you so much already. If you'd assigned another officer to the Hampshire case, Vee and I would never have met."

CHAPTER 3

Feeling like the cat with the cream, and hoping that feeling wasn't showing in his face, Bryce took the stairs to the CID general office. Sergeant Haig was at his desk, head down, working on a statement. He jumped to his feet when he realised his boss was standing over him.

"We need to have a chat," said Bryce to his colleague, "come upstairs."

Haig knew his boss well enough to see that something important was afoot, and wondered what the 'chat' was to be about. His presence before the Chief Inspector was usually arranged by telephone. Occasionally, he might go upstairs to bring something to Bryce's attention. The Scottish Sergeant couldn't ever remember his boss visiting the CID department before.

"Shut the door and take a seat," said Bryce when they arrived in his office.

Haig looked expectantly at his chief, and noticed he was now wearing a huge smile. "Something amusing happened, sir?" he enquired.

"Amusing? Not as such, but something that I'm sure will make you smile too.

"I was summoned to a meeting with the Commissioner a few minutes ago, and learned four things – at least three of which affect you directly.

"First, I'm to become Chief Superintendent with immediate effect."

Haig, spontaneous and sincere with his congratulations, was not at all surprised by the news. "I said you'd be moving on before me!"

"Well no, not really. You see, as of now, you become Detective Inspector. You'll get the formal notice tomorrow."

It was Haig's turn to be astonished. "Thank you, sir. Whatever good word you've put in for me has obviously worked!"

"Not at all – you've earned it yourself. You can tell Fiona tonight, of course, but otherwise keep it to yourself until you get your letter of appointment tomorrow.

"And promotions aren't the only changes in the pipeline." Bryce relayed the information he had just received about the retirements, and the restructuring they had precipitated. "I've been assured that my post isn't expected to be a full-time desk job. I'm to be allowed to roll my sleeves up and join you in the field occasionally."

"Aye, well I can see why you were smiling now, sir. And I'm certainly doing the same!"

"Before we move on to the detail of our

new case, there's one more thing for you to seriously consider. If you feel like a bit more independence, it might be possible to get you a transfer as a DI in one of the divisions. Only you can decide whether that might help your career in the longer term. Think about that over the next couple of days, and let me know."

Haig almost flung his head from side to side. "No, I don't need to think about it at all, sir. If you'll have me, I'd like to stay."

Bryce grinned and made an exaggerated gesture of helplessness. "Looks like I'm lumbered with you then! Let me tell you about our new case."

The Chief Superintendent gave his Inspector the gist of what he had been told half an hour earlier. Haig whistled.

"You'd better dust the Bishop's letter and envelope before we actually read it. I don't want anyone else to know about this yet, so fetch your bag of tricks up here to check for prints.

"While you're doing that I'll read the Commissioner's notes."

***

Caspar Charrington's letter comprised a single typed sheet of paper, and it didn't take long for Haig to finish his task.

"One set of prints on the letter, sir, presumably the Bishop's own," he reported. "Several partial sets on the envelope, including the Bishop's again."

Bryce came around the table to read the letter over Haig's shoulder. Typed on a machine with a somewhat smudged typeface on commonly-available azure paper, it had been enclosed in a matching envelope addressed to The Right Reverend Caspar Charrington, c/o The Goring Hotel, Beeston Place, SW1, marked Strictly Private and Personal, and dated 29th October 1950.

My Lord

Adverse and distressing reports have reached me, regarding your conduct. Let me mention two instances.

Years ago, before your preferment, you were the Vicar of Blyth Magna in Dorset. While the incumbent of that parish, you sold, without lawful authority, various items of church plate. I have the dates, the details of the silverware, and the amount for which each piece was sold.

Not long after your elevation to the bishopric, you accepted a bribe of two hundred pounds to appoint to a benefice a man whom you knew to be wholly unsuitable for the office. In other words you are guilty of simony, which I understand has been an offence since 1588. Again, I know the date, the name, the position, and the reasons why your appointee would never have received the post were it not for your intervention.

I feel sure that you would wish to avoid any

unpleasant and humiliating revelations reaching the Archbishop and the Monarch.

To that end, you may care to contribute to a fund into which sinners may make a payment in expiation. The equivalent, if you like, of the way a fine issued by a court clears the slate. Shall we say one thousand pounds?

I cannot emphasise too strongly that it would be extremely detrimental to your position were you to approach, discuss, or involve anyone else in this matter – anyone at all.

You will, I am sure, understand why I have not felt able to supply my address.

I am, most sincerely,
Your Nemesis

The DCS returned to his chair with no comment other than "Hmm". He pushed the Commissioner's notes over for Haig to read, and sat staring into space.

"I'll summarise what we have so far," said Bryce when the Sergeant had finished reading. "We can probably assume that the other two are on the same sort of paper and in the same tone. All are from someone who styles himself 'Nemesis'.

"First, the Bishop. He's accused of simony, and of selling Church silver.

"Frankly, I'll need to refresh my memory on canon law, but despite the reference to an ancient law I think all this would come under a nineteenth century Benefices Act. I doubt if either allegation would be dealt with in the ordinary criminal courts; but blackmail is definitely a criminal matter, so that's our remit.

Haig nodded. "Aye, but here, sir," he pointed to a paragraph, "the way the figure of a thousand pounds is suggested – rather than demanded – reads oddly to me." He quoted from the letter: "'*you may care to contribute*'. It's more like shaking a charity collecting can under the Bishop's nose, rather than an outright demand for money."

"Yes, it's oblique, but hardly subtle," agreed the DCS. "On that basis alone I believe we're dealing with someone who is not only educated, but possibly uses words as a tool of his trade."

Bryce picked up the notes made by the Commissioner during his telephone conversations. "Lord Hartley is accused of using privileged information to make a great deal of money buying and selling stocks. His demand is for five, rather than one thousand pounds, but the menace is still there: the writer will inform all the newspapers. Five thousand may only be petty cash to his lordship, but it's a great deal of money given that he doesn't appear to have broken any sort of written law.

"As far as Poole is concerned, the allegation is that during the last war he accepted substantial but unspecified bribes from at least three different companies, following which he lobbied tirelessly on their behalf in order to get them lucrative Government contracts. At the time of the first alleged bribe he was only a backbench MP, but he'd become a junior minister by the time of the next two."

"Lobbying isn't an offence, though," observed Haig.

"No, not as such. It goes on in the corridors of power every day. Poole's '*contribution*' for the author's silence is also five thousand pounds. Again, it probably won't be a large amount to him, but it's a sizeable demand, nevertheless.

"And you're right; neither Hartley nor Poole, as far as we can see, has committed any offence; each has allegedly only done what many men of their ilk do. And when the Bishop spoke to the Commissioner he refuted the allegations against him. Yet Nemesis expects all of them to pay enormous sums to keep quiet."

"Do you expect further allegations to justify the demands, then, sir?" asked Haig.

Bryce leaned back in his chair and stared up at the ceiling. "Yes. I think that even grubbier matters will soon emerge," he said. "Nemesis actually says '*let me mention two instances*', which could imply that he knows of others. Also, and I may be reading too much into this, the sentence '*I'm sure you would wish to avoid any unpleasant and humiliating revelations*' could be a hint that the revelations might not be restricted to what's already been mentioned. And the other two letters apparently include the same or similar wording. It seems to me that the existing 'revelations' aren't sufficiently *'unpleasant and humiliating'* to warrant such large payments – certainly not in the cases of Poole and Hartley."

"Nemesis won't just be satisfied with a one-off payment either, I guess," remarked Haig.

"I'm sure you're right." Bryce sat forward again. "I haven't had many dealings with blackmailers, but I understand that those who only expect a single payment and then retire quietly are very rare birds. Once a victim has made the initial payment, he's dangling on the hook for as long as the blackmailer can keep him there and take more slices off him. If I'm right about there being innuendos in the Bishop's letter, then I think we'll see the same in the other two letters, and I'm quite sure the intention will be to escalate matters."

"What about the 'menaces' bit, sir?"

"Well, it's clear enough in the Bishop's letter. Pay up, or I'll tell the Archbishop and the King about you. According to the Commissioner's notes, the threat to Poole is to tell his constituency officials, the Prime Minister, and the newspapers. And the papers are to be informed about Hartley. All definite menaces.

"But with or without additional demands, or additional allegations, there's something missing from this first letter."

Haig re-read the missive and gave himself

a silent kicking as he realised what his boss meant. "There will have to be follow-up communications, because Nemesis doesn't say how the money is to be paid?"

"Exactly. The final matter of significance in the Bishop's letter, and recorded for the other two men in the Commissioner's notes, is that all three are told that if they contact anyone else at all – which clearly means the police – their chance to buy the blackmailer's silence is forfeited, and they will be exposed." Bryce sat back again and folded his arms. "What's the first thing we need to do, Inspector?"

"Establish all the connections between the three, sir."

"Yes. We can start with the fact that they all wander around the Palace of Westminster in their various roles. Beyond that, what friends – or enemies – they may have in common; and who could have been in a position to acquire the information. There's something else here which may be significant. The Bishop's letter isn't addressed to his palace in Crewe, it's sent to a London hotel – where he was in fact staying. So the blackmailer is *au fait* with his victim's current movements.

"My first job is to set up meetings with each of them. You go back downstairs for now, and carry on with whatever you were doing. I'll call you back when I've made a few arrangements."

The Commissioner had noted the necessary private telephone numbers, and as the door closed behind the Inspector, Bryce picked up his receiver and started making calls. The task took some time. Eventually, he put down the external telephone handset and picked up the internal instead and spoke to Haig.

"I've made an appointment with Hartley. He has a permanent suite at the Savoy, and he'll see us at two o'clock today. He's understandably anxious about not being seen with the police in case the blackmailer finds out he's breaking the '*no contact*' condition; so we're to announce ourselves as Messrs Wilson and Trent."

Haig made no comment, but wondered whether adopting an alias would prevent observant newspaper readers from identifying the DCS, given that his picture had been published more than once following a successful case.

"I've fixed up with the other two as well," continued Bryce. "David Poole will see us in his room in the Commons at four thirty this afternoon.

"The Bishop is indeed in London. I'm glad of that – it'd take us all day to get to his See and back. He regularly stays at the Goring, which partially explains how the letter reached him. He's completely tied up today, but we're expected in the hotel at a quarter to eleven tomorrow.

"Charrington says he can only spare an

hour, as he has a lunch meeting in the House of Lords. While he didn't suggest the equivalent of Wilson and Trent, he was clearly concerned about our involvement, so I've told both him and Poole that those will be our names whenever we make contact through their staff or third parties.

"Let's walk along the Embankment to the Savoy this afternoon. I'll see you downstairs at one-forty."

CHAPTER 4

The two detectives turned left out of Scotland Yard, and walked briskly through the Victoria Embankment Gardens, one of London's many pleasant and verdant areas of escape from the proximity of trams and other traffic. The weather was mild for the time of year, and the walk made a change from going everywhere by car or public transport. Arriving level with the Savoy, and noting they were several minutes ahead of schedule, Bryce decided to go up Carting Lane to the hotel's front entrance.

This was Haig's first visit to the prestigious establishment, and although he had travelled along the Strand many times he had never before noted the oddity which he now saw as they turned into Savoy Court. The traffic here drove on the 'wrong' side of the road. Seeing the surprise on his face, Bryce explained.

"Apart from one or two bus stations, this is the only place in London with this arrangement. Some say that it started so that hackney drivers could reach to open the door on the right-hand side as they pulled up at the hotel, without needing to get down from the carriage – female passengers apparently sat on the right behind the driver.

"A more probable theory is that it's to stop cabs, pulling up at the Savoy Theatre on the right-hand side, from forming a queue and blocking the hotel entrance at the end. Also, the cabbies, as they drew away again, could perhaps pick up a fare as they went on to the turn-around bit in front of the hotel.

"There's a legend that there was a special Act of Parliament granting this right, but I don't think that's true. It's actually a private road, not a public highway, so I can't see that a dispensation has ever been needed."

Haig reflected that since he had worked with his current boss, not many days had passed without his picking up some little-known but interesting fact.

A doorman, resplendent in his uniform, greeted them with a bow and gave a starting push to one of the huge revolving doors. The two officers arrived at the reception desk and informed the clerk that Messrs Wilson and Trent had an appointment with Lord Hartley.

"Certainly, gentlemen, he is expecting you in the Victoria Suite – I'll get someone to take you up."

"No, don't bother," said 'Mr Wilson', "we'll find our own way."

"As you wish, sir. It's on the third floor."

The suite door was opened by a man approaching forty, clean-shaven, with short dark hair and steel-framed spectacles. From the peer's many pictures in the newspapers, the detectives knew that this was not Lord Hartley.

Douglas Burnett introduced himself as his lordship's Principal Private Secretary, before ushering them through the hallway to the living area of the suite. Here, the man whom they expected to meet was sitting at a table almost buried under papers.

In his early seventies, tall, heavily-built, with a crown of thick grey hair, Lord Hartley in person was very like his press photographs – with the exception of his face, which was extremely florid when seen in the flesh rather than in newsprint.

His lordship didn't rise to greet them.

"Sit down, gentlemen," he told the Yard officers, before telling his secretary, "Disappear for an hour, Burnett, would you; very private matter to discuss."

The Secretary nodded, collected a dark grey coat, scarf and trilby from a nearby chair, and left the suite.

Introductions were made, after which Hartley came straight to the point. "You'll want to see the letter I received." He held out a large, unaddressed and unsealed envelope.

Bryce opened the end and peered inside

before gently shaking out the blackmail letter and its envelope onto the only square foot of open space on the table. Haig stood beside him and the two detectives silently read the peer's missive.

"We'll take these with us and check them for prints," said Bryce, "but frankly, without much optimism. I assume your Secretary handled the envelope, but not the letter?"

"Correct; although as it happens I'd be quite happy for Burnett to see it. The only reason I haven't said anything to him is because I've always understood that in a case of blackmail the fewer people who know about it, the better.

"I have three secretaries, and the rule is that they are never to open any correspondence marked 'Private' or 'Personal'. Envelopes marked 'Confidential' are okay."

His lordship poked a finger at the letter and addressed the allegations it contained. "Regarding the content, I don't deny I used that sort of information when buying and selling shares. Nothing improper; and certainly nothing illegal." His voice rose. "If this rogue thinks I'm going to pay thousands of pounds to stop him publishing that drivel, he's barking mad and can be damned into the bargain!"

"I see your point, m'lord," said Bryce, "but I wonder if you read anything between the lines? Looking at this, and taking into account your no doubt correct belief that the present accusations are 'drivel', I suspect that there's an extra hidden threat among the well-crafted sentences."

His lordship looked blank. "What are you suggesting, Chief Superintendent?"

"I think it's just possible that the writer is giving a hint – 'I have more information; and this is only a first instalment of what I shall reveal about you'."

Hartley's face reddened further. "I hadn't read it like that myself, but I suppose it could be seen that way."

"I also take into account the level of the demand when I suggest there may be something more to come," said Bryce. "As you rightly say, you aren't accused of any criminal offence. So, I must ask myself, what makes the author think that you would even contemplate submitting to this level of extortion and paying up – unless he supplies further, and more damaging matters, to justify his price?"

Lord Hartley was not to be drawn on the point of further revelations. "I have no intention of paying, regardless of what this Nemesis scoundrel thinks he can reveal about me," he growled.

"Quite," agreed Bryce, "and at the moment you couldn't pay, even if you were minded to, because so far our correspondent hasn't told you how to do so. No doubt that will come later. I need hardly say that you must contact us as soon as any form of communication arrives – it won't necessarily be another letter.

"As for this first allegation against you; are we talking about multiple share dealings over a number of years?"

Hartley nodded. "Yes, I suppose so. I've been a director of numerous companies since the Great War, and apart from that I have a wide circle of friends and acquaintances; I'm a member of two London clubs, for example. I pick up bits of information nearly every day. Some is useful; most isn't. I'm adept at sifting the wheat from the chaff, and then I buy and sell – shares, futures, bonds, whatever – accordingly."

"How long have Douglas Burnett and your other private secretaries been with you, my lord?" asked Haig, who was making notes in his pocketbook.

"Burnett joined me in 1931, immediately after coming down from university. His father had worked for me since 1913, so I've known Douglas since he was a nipper. He had an RNVR commission, and went off during the war to serve in minesweepers. He came back to me in 1945, and two years ago he stepped up to Principal Secretary when his father retired. Both of them highly intelligent, highly educated, and above all, trustworthy.

"The others are Jeremy Middleton and Alan Curtis. Like the Burnett's they're also from good families. Good schools and colleges, too. They've both been with me for about four years.

"Incidentally, I'm very old-fashioned; I don't employ women on this sort of work. Nor am I a cheapskate; all my staff are paid well above the market rate. I can't see that any of them have reason to resort to blackmail."

"What about when you buy shares, and so on; do you always use the same broker?" asked Haig.

"No, I don't. I deal with several. I'll give you their details, of course, but again, I can see no reason why any of them would stoop to this. They're all well-heeled men themselves, and if any one of them felt he could point a finger at me I'm quite sure I could reciprocate!"

Hartley listed names on a notepad, tore off the sheet and pushed it across the table.

"Any other people, domestic servants, friends, or relatives even, who would be aware of your use of privileged information?" asked the DCS.

The peer gave this question more thought than he had the previous questions before firmly stating: "Certainly not any friends or relatives in my home. I have a soundproof study in my house, and outside that room I never, ever, discuss business. My wife won't have business talk at the table, and since I don't smoke we don't do any of that ladies withdrawing nonsense after we've eaten with company. But that's no hardship, as I prefer my evenings with conversation about any other topic." He shook his head. "No; no visitor could have heard anything over a meal.

"In my clubs and in the Lords I listen a lot, but I don't talk much. I never do business deals there, nor ever talk about what I'm planning to buy or sell."

Hartley glanced over at Haig to see if he was keeping up. Deciding that he was, he continued. "I have a valet, but he rarely has any need to see me in my study. My butler might come in occasionally, and a footman or other servant even less frequently. But that said, I really can't see that any of them would be present long enough to pick up any information that would make any sense to them if I happened to be on the telephone. Someone comes in to clean the room when I'm out, of course. But all of my drawers have locks, and I make use of them.

"As for fellow board members – current colleagues and ex-colleagues – there are many who might easily know of my holdings. But since we're all similar men, I'm quite sure they conduct themselves as I do."

Bryce considered all this and made a decision. "I gather that when you spoke to the Commissioner he was circumspect, and didn't tell you certain other facts. I've decided that I need to pass on some of this information, because otherwise it may be impossible to find the blackmailer.

"On the same day that you received

your demand, two more men received almost identical letters. All three of you have a presence in the Palace of Westminster. That's a significant link which I'm hoping will assist in narrowing the field of suspects."

Hartley gazed at him in surprise. "Three of us, all in Westminster? Good God! Who are the others then?"

"This is in strict confidence, naturally," said Bryce. "The Bishop of Crewe and David Poole."

Although Hartley was surprised to learn he was not the only victim, the Yard detectives noticed he seemed unsurprised when he heard the names of his co-accused.

"I've met Poole a few times over the years. He's a member of one of my clubs; wouldn't say I know him at all well, though.

"As a fellow crossbench peer I often see Charrington, but I'm an agnostic so I have nothing in common with the man. Or at least I shouldn't have thought so, beyond the fact that we now share the same blackmailer."

Hartley's manner became forceful. "What does Nemesis say these two have been doing, eh? I think I'm entitled to know whether Poole and Charrington have been more – or less – smeared than I have!"

"It's neither fair nor necessary to tell you that, m'lord. What I can say is that one of the other two letters carries a similar veiled implication of further revelations. We haven't seen the third letter yet.

Hartley wasn't pleased with Bryce's mild rebuffing of his demand for additional information. His tone became more aggressive. "Well, if you're going to be difficult I shall get the information directly out of the Commissioner instead!"

"I think not, m'lord. You'll find the Commissioner won't take your call or deal with any other form of communication from you. Inspector Haig and I are your contacts now," replied Bryce.

Hartley's inarticulate response and the look he gave the detectives expressed his displeasure. Privately thinking that he would certainly approach the Commissioner again, if he felt so inclined, the peer decided to continue with the Yard officers for the present.

"Well, as I say, I'm not a friend of either of the other two. Neither has ever been to my house nor I to theirs. In the club, I've never dined with Poole, nor even stood at the bar with him for a drink, as far as I recall. And Charrington, to be blunt, isn't someone I'd want to have a drink with under any circumstances.

"Nevertheless," Hartley continued, "our blackmailer-in-common must have some tangible connection with the three of us. That fact alone must narrow things down and eliminate millions of people for you." His lordship spoke as though he had singlehandedly – and very considerably – reduced the burden of the investigation for the policemen.

"That's true," agreed Bryce pleasantly, before firmly disabusing the peer, "but until we find that connection we can't eliminate any of those millions, unfortunately."

The Chief Superintendent and his Inspector prepared to leave.

"We won't take up any more of your time m'lord. Please think again about how you might be connected to the Bishop and Mr Poole, and contact us at the Yard when you hear further from Nemesis."

***

The two detectives retraced their steps towards their base.

"Not very enlightening, sir," remarked Haig. "And although I veer towards agnosticism myself, I don't fancy a drink at the bar with Hartley either – not that he's ever likely to offer me one!"

Bryce grinned. "No. Can't say I warmed to the man. And I think trading off the back of privileged information should be made illegal; the sooner the better. It'll be interesting to see how similar, or different, the other two men are compared with Hartley. There has to be something to connect these people – other than all being Westminster habitués."

"What you said about the Commissioner not accepting his calls; did you make that up, sir?"

"No, certainly not," laughed Bryce. "The Commissioner anticipated something of the kind, and said I could tell any of these gentlemen that he wouldn't deal with them again."

"We need to look into all his stockbrokers, and especially his private secretaries, sir, since they presumably action his lordship's instructions," said Haig.

"Absolutely. But before we get back to the Yard and make a start on that, let's have a cup of tea to celebrate our promotions," suggested the DCS.

The two men set off along the Strand. Passing an ABC café, they looked at each other. Without either needing to speak, they turned and went inside. Over a cup of tea and a slice of fruit cake, Bryce remarked on the two principal chains of cafeterias in London.

"Interesting history, the Aerated Bread Company. Not as many outlets as Lyons, and not spread across the country to the same extent, although I believe they did open sites in America and Australia at one time. And even the ordinary Lyons restaurants are rather more upmarket – the Corner Houses particularly so, of course. But there must be a huge demand for this sort of place in London – especially in the West End. I walked from St Pauls to Charing Cross, recently, and for some unknown reason counted the ABCs as I went along. There's one on Ludgate Hill, two in Fleet Street, and five in the Strand – plus the one in Charing Cross station. That's nine in a mile and a half, although they don't all have seating. Might be worth buying some shares – I bet Hartley holds some!"

Haig grinned. "Me, I've always felt more at home in an ABC than in a Lyons," he said, "but perhaps it'll be different now I've got pips on my shoulders. As for the number of customers, I bet the Corner House just along the street probably seats as many as all the nine ABCs together!"

CHAPTER 5

Four o'clock saw the two officers walking the short distance to Parliament. Bryce, who had been a guest in the House of Commons before, led the way to the Parliament Square gate and into New Palace Yard. A uniformed police sergeant, who recognised the DCS without needing identification, called to a constable nearby.

The detectives were taken up a flight of stairs and along a lengthy corridor where their guide stopped, indicating that they had reached the room required. Thanking him, Bryce knocked. A muffled 'enter' could just be heard through the thick oak door.

As with Peregrine Hartley, both detectives had seen photographs of the cabinet minister in the newspapers. Of the three almost identically dressed men sitting at a table, they immediately recognised which was Poole. In his early fifties, he was at least fifteen years older than his companions. Well-tailored and most distinguished, the Minister's straight-backed bearing and rather haughty facial expression could easily have marked him out as an aristocrat, or even minor royalty.

All three men rose, Poole's associates gathering up their papers preparatory to leaving.

"Come in, gentlemen," said the Minister, inviting the visitors to take the seats vacated by his staff.

"Those men were my Parliamentary Private Secretary, and my Principal Private Secretary," explained Poole. "They know nothing of why you're here; the letter went to my home, and I opened it personally. I didn't even show my wife.

"This really is an utterly stinking kettle of fish," he continued irritably. "I have no previous experience of blackmail, other than cases I might read about in the newspapers. You'll want to see the letter, of course."

Like Lord Hartley, Poole had put both letter and envelope inside a larger envelope, which he took out of his briefcase and passed over to Bryce. Easing the contents out as before, the DCS carefully spread open the letter. The two policemen read it in silence.

At first sight, this letter and envelope were exactly the same as the other two. Neatly typed, with the envelope correctly addressed to *The Right Honourable David Poole, MP*. The letter was unsigned, but closed, like the other two, with the valediction '*Your Nemesis*'.

The content was just as the Commissioner's note had stated. But both officers saw the supplementary implication about *'unpleasant revelations'* was almost identical to that in the other two letters.

Bryce raised this point first.

"I hadn't noticed that, Chief Superintendent," said Poole, "and I still don't read it that way. We'll have to see. If your interpretation is correct, I wonder what the hell else my Nemesis thinks I might have been up to!"

"As you say, time will tell, Minister. He will have to contact you again in order to explain how the demand is to be paid."

"Yes, I understand that. I'll let you know as soon as anything else arrives. However, I maintain that I've done nothing unlawful in my promotion of various companies, and it goes without saying that I have no intention of shovelling my money towards this criminal!"

"Indeed," said Bryce. "Presumably there must be a good number of people who are aware of your lobbying?"

"Yes, inevitably. I freely admit that over the years I was paid by companies, to speak on their behalf in the Commons and in Whitehall. Most MPs and some civil servants would know of my lobbying; and they'd have to be desperately dense if they didn't realise that I was being paid for my vigorous efforts. It certainly wouldn't be difficult for a lot of people to discover that about me."

Poole considered aloud others with the necessary knowledge. "The directors of the companies concerned would also know, of course, and no doubt some of their senior staff. A few of my close friends – all, as it happens, MPs – absolutely know for sure, because we've occasionally discussed this over the years. My bank manager and some of his staff might see the incoming payments and also draw conclusions."

Inspector Haig, once again recording key points, asked, "What about at home, Minister; do you ever discuss business matters there?"

"Yes, I entertain frequently; it's expected of me. Very mixed bag of guests at my table; politicians, mandarins, businessmen – all sorts.

"After dinner, when the ladies have withdrawn and a good vintage port has lubricated everyone, and the cigars are drawing nicely, the discussion will often turn to ways of earning money. But that sort of conversation would depend on who the guests are, naturally."

"What about at your club?"

"Again, yes. Like most politicians, I'm a fairly convivial chap anyway, but socialising would go with the job even if I wasn't. I can't remember discussing lobbying in particular, but I'm sure the topic will have cropped up over the years."

Poole changed direction. "A few minutes

ago you said 'he', Chief Superintendent. Are you confident there aren't female blackmailers?"

"I don't have any statistics to hand," said Bryce, "but I believe there are such instances. Spurned mistresses, for example; trying to extract some money by threatening to tell wives about their husband's affairs."

"Won't happen in my case!" was Poole's blunt rebuttal.

The detectives noted that the Minister didn't clarify his remark by explaining whether this was because he didn't keep any mistresses, or because he wouldn't deign to mention business to them if he did. Given Poole's statement that no business talk took place in his house until after the ladies had withdrawn, both privately decided it was probably the latter.

"Incidentally, my connection with three of the companies goes back seven or eight years, and I no longer have an agreement with them; one has since closed down."

Poole drew forward a sheet of paper and uncapped his fountain pen. "Let me just give you something about people who definitely know some details."

The minister spent the next few minutes writing.

"Best I can do off the top of my head," he said as he handed Bryce his notes. "However, apart from the fact that there may be many more that haven't come to mind, few if any of these people would be aware of more than a couple of my corporate sponsors."

"While I glance through your list, Minister, Inspector Haig will tell you something else."

Poole looked towards Haig.

"It seems you aren't the only target of Nemesis, sir," began the DI. "We know of two more who received similar letters on the same day as you – the Bishop of Crewe, and Lord Hartley."

"Hell's teeth!" exclaimed the MP. "What are they supposed to have done?"

Haig shook his head. "We can't tell you that, sir. But as all three of you have roles in Westminster, we hope that some mutual acquaintance may emerge. With three victims, there must be a higher chance of finding the culprit than if there was only one isolated victim."

Poole was quick to take the point. "Yes, I see that, and let's hope you're right, Inspector. My circle is by no means limited to members of my political party, but even so, most friends are political animals of one sort or another – which is why I can't think of any connection between myself and Caspar Charrington. I only know him by sight really; I don't recall ever speaking to him.

"I don't know Peregrine Hartley much better; we're not close in any way. Hartley is apolitical; perhaps even anti-political. I've been at a few functions when he was present, and we're members of the same club, although I can't remember ever speaking to him there.

"I suppose it's likely, inevitable almost, that we have mutual acquaintances, but I don't see how on earth you could ascertain who they are. Suppose each of the three of us drew up a list of fifty acquaintances. Given that we move in different circles, I doubt if there would be more than one person who appeared on all three lists. And he'd probably have nothing to do with this anyway!"

Bryce had finished reading Poole's list of names and looked up to acknowledge the Minister's observation. "That's right. We also have to accept that it's just possible, however unlikely, that the Westminster connection is coincidental.

"Anyway, Minister, if you think of more names, or you have any ideas, or you receive a further communication, please telephone Scotland Yard at once."

***

"Time to go home," said Bryce to Haig as they left the building. "Do you need to go back to the office?"

"No, guv," said Haig, automatically slipping into informal mode at the end of the working day. I'll drop into the tube station and go and tell Fiona the news. And thank you once more."

"All merited, Alex, and no thanks needed. I've come by car today, so I'll get back to the Yard and then go on home to give Veronica the glad tidings. I think we might celebrate tonight.

"Speaking of glad tidings and celebrations, Vee and I have some even better news – we're expecting a baby next March. I only learned about it last night."

"Congratulations again, guv! Please pass on my good wishes to Mrs Bryce."

"I will. It's early days, of course, and things can go wrong. Still, it's an understatement if I tell you we're both extremely happy right now!

"Oh, and while we're in informal mode, drop the 'Mrs Bryce' – she's always Veronica to you and Fiona, Alex."

The detectives parted on their customary good terms, each appreciating that working life was much more pleasant without internecine bickering and rivalry.

***

As anticipated, Veronica and Fiona were very happy indeed to hear their respective husband's news.

The additional money wouldn't mean much to the affluent Bryces. Nor did the improvement in status with his new rank mean overmuch to Bryce himself. But for Veronica, the very early promotion was important for a different reason: it was further demonstration (as if that were needed) of the fact that Philip was appreciated in high places, and that he might one day reach the very top – where she firmly believed he belonged.

The couple agreed a meal and a West End show would be enjoyable, and Bryce made the arrangements as Veronica went to change.

Before attempting to secure a table anywhere for dinner, he made a quick telephone call to the ticket office of the Phoenix Theatre in Charing Cross Road. Enquiring if there had been any returned tickets for the evening's performance, he was delighted to secure two excellent seats for '*Dear Miss Phoebe*'. Veronica was very keen on musical theatre, and he knew she wanted to see how the libretto and score of this new production dealt with J. M Barrie's original work, '*Quality Street*', on which it was based.

With a table booked at *The Ivy*, Bryce felt their double celebration was being well and memorably marked. He belatedly wished he'd thought to buy some of the confectionery named after Barrie's play, but told himself Veronica would be just as happy without the sweets.

For Alex and Fiona Haig, both money and status were important. In common with others on lower incomes, all extra pay would be noticeable. Haig calculated that his promotion should mean an increase of perhaps twenty percent immediately, and with annual increments he could look forward to a higher ceiling eventually. By way of celebration, he suggested that they ask an obliging neighbour to come in to look after their daughter Rosie on Saturday evening, so that Fiona and he could go out for a fish supper followed by a film at the Gaumont or the Regal – two treats which they could never normally enjoy on the same day.

The Haigs spent the rest of their evening talking over the possibility of buying a house instead of renting. When the calculations for that conversation were concluded with a favourable outcome, they sat together with the evening paper Haig had picked up on the tube, and considered the cinema choices for their weekend outing.

CHAPTER 6

Thursday 2nd November, 1950

Bryce arrived at the Yard early. His promotion, and the new investigation which had come with it, didn't alter the fact that he had existing responsibilities. He intended to spend a good hour on those before considering his new case again.

He was surprised when the officer on duty at the door advised him that Patrick Anderson-Hall wanted to see him immediately. Thinking that his senior officer didn't usually get into the building so far ahead of time, he thanked the Sergeant and bounded up the two flights of stairs to the AC's room. There was nobody in the outer office, and the inner door was open. He stood in the doorway and tapped on the frame.

"Ah, come in, Philip. I have news on your blackmail cases. Take a pew.

"It seems our three so far are not the only ones. We now know of two more. I had a call at home at seven o'clock this morning from the Chief Constable of Kent. It seems a prosperous

Tonbridge local, Julian Barratt, used his own shotgun to kill himself last night. Divorced chap; lived alone apart from a couple of servants. Semi-retired, I gather, with various business interests.

"The officer looking into the death couldn't find a suicide note, but he did find a blackmail letter laying open on the desk. Barratt was accused of corruption; specifically that he had colluded with a certain peer of the realm."

Bryce raised his eyebrows. "Lord Hartley?"

Anderson-Hall nodded. "The very same. As the allegation was so serious and involved a peer, the Kent Chief decided to get the Yard involved straight away. So that case is ours too.

"And that's not the worst of it. Yesterday evening, a valet was shot dead in Mortlake. Name of Terence Crossland. No dispute as to who shot him because his employer, Stuart Galbraith, immediately admitted it.

"He said that Crossland was trying to blackmail him. The police found another of the blackmail letters in Galbraith's study.

"On a whim, the local DI mentioned it to his mentor – our soon-to-retire Chief Super, Tommy Burrell. Tommy tried two or three times to get hold of you last night, but presumably you were out celebrating?"

Bryce nodded.

"He was going away for a few days first thing this morning, so he gave up on you and called me. I've already spoken to DI Haynes myself, and he's expecting someone to see him at Putney today."

The AC paused to let Bryce speak.

"That's five letters now, sir. Barratt allegedly has a connection with Hartley, but do we know of any link between Galbraith and any of the others?"

"No idea. I don't even know what Galbraith does – or did – for a living, and how that might tie in with any of the others. Both Tommy and I are just messengers in all this. Have you seen the first three yet?"

"Poole and Hartley, yes. The Bishop isn't available until later this morning.

"Given that in at least two of the letters there is no suggestion of criminality, sir, I'm fairly sure that the blackmailer has further information which he's holding back.

"What I'm not at all convinced about is whether new letters – if they contain more damaging accusations – will be passed on to us."

***

Bryce found Haig waiting in his office.

"I heard on the grapevine that the AC had asked for you, and concluded that there must be more developments."

"The grapevine, and your conclusion, are both accurate," laughed Bryce. "Take a seat." In a few sentences, he passed on the new information. "This is getting too big for the two of us. Who can we rope in from CID to help?"

"DS Cole, and DCs Kittow and Drummond were downstairs a minute ago, sir. But I don't know what they're working on at the moment."

"What about Yapp?"

Haig shook his head. "Problem there, sir. You must have just missed seeing DCI Webber on his way to the AC's office. Whilst you were in your meeting, Yapp was accused of taking bribes. Mr Webber arrested him in the CID room and charged him there and then with an offence under the Public Bodies Corrupt Practices Act."

"I knew there was a suspicion a few months ago that someone was giving tip-offs ahead of raids. Why did they think it was Yapp?"

"Mr Webber set a trap. He personally swore the information for the search warrant. Only he, Yapp, and the Magistrate knew about the raid planned for two nights ago. Four uniformed men were brought in from another division at an hour's notice, and were only told the target when they were a street away. You can probably guess the rest," said Haig.

"Squeaky clean premises?" offered Bryce.

"Completely. The raid netted nothing apart from a big cheesy smile from Jack Hall, the owner, and a slow handclap from half a dozen of his cronies who ostensibly 'work' at his depot. Hall was that cocky he offered to 'Put the kettle on for you, Mr Webber, an' all your brave boys. Where would we all be wivout your heroic protecshun?'."

Bryce smiled at Haig's rendition of a Cockney accent. It wasn't the first time he'd heard it, and he thought it was extremely good. "I take it that put a lot of salt on Mr Webber's tail," he said.

Haig nodded. "He was livid. He went back with one of the visiting officers yesterday evening and got Hall on his own – you know how very persuasive Mr Webber can be, sir," he said, meaningfully. "He told us just now that Hall quickly admitted he'd bribed Yapp. Gave him the name of a witness, too.

"This morning, Mr Webber stormed into the general office, told Yapp he had cast iron proof he'd taken a £200 bribe, suspended him from duty, and charged him there and then. Yapp didn't make any denial, and watching his face there's no doubt of his guilt."

"Then he's a complete fool and I'm disappointed in him," said Bryce. "He could have got on in the Force.

"So without him, then, we're left with Cole, Drummond, and Kittow to choose from. Cole retires next week, and should never have made sergeant anyway – he hasn't the brain. We won't use him. I don't know Drummond. Have you worked with him?"

"No, sir, he's very new. Transferred from one of the divisions a few weeks ago and he'd only moved out of uniform a year before that.

He's a personable lad, though, and from what I've seen of him in the office, he's quick and keen. First name is Gerry, by the way.

"Good. We'll take him, and Kittow. Go and see who they're working for at present and try and square filching them away. Pull rank – yours if possible, mine if necessary. Don't mention the Commissioner's imprimatur in all of this unless you really have to. Then tell those two they've been press-ganged, and bring them up here."

Haig had hardly left the room when the telephone rang. Bryce picked up the receiver, confirmed who he was, and listened silently for the next minute, making notes as he did so. He asked several questions and made more notes as each was answered.

"Either I or one of my officers will come and see you as soon as convenient. Good. Let's say between three and four. Thank you."

He replaced the handset and sat contemplating his ceiling again until he was interrupted by the arrival of Haig and the two detective constables. Bryce rose, nodding a friendly greeting to Kittow.

"We've not met before, Constable; welcome," he said, shaking Drummond's hand, much to the officer's surprise.

"Pull up a chair, everyone.

"Do these two know about our changes in ranks?" he enquired of Haig.

"Doubt it sir; I've said nothing."

"Okay. Well, gentlemen, this is the first day of a new era in CID. Mr Haig here is now an inspector, and I'm a chief superintendent. There will be a number of other changes in the next few weeks – a new department, in effect. But we'll leave all of that for another day.

"Our task in hand is a blackmail case. Or at least it was until a few hours ago, because now we have a murder mixed in, and a suicide."

Bryce gave the two DCs the essential details of the case and added, "But during the time Mr Haig was downstairs fetching you two, there's been yet another development.

"A Dr Simon Marlowe rang a few minutes ago. He received a similar letter yesterday. That makes six that we know about. His first thought was to chuck it on the fire, as the allegations of plagiarism it contains are, he says, arrant nonsense. He decided to report it because, and I quote, 'blackmailers shouldn't be allowed to get away with it'."

"Did he also have the Commissioner's ear, sir?" asked Haig.

"No. This chap doesn't have such a high profile as the first three we heard of – he's a palaeontologist. Lives in St John's Wood. He said he wasn't sure if his local police station dealt with things like this, so he called the Yard. Yesterday, I told the switchboard and post room supervisors to make sure everyone downstairs knew to pass anything blackmail-related to me in the first instance.

"We have a lot to do, and we'll have to work individually to get it all done."

Fresh pages were turned over in pocketbooks as the Chief Superintendent shared out the tasks.

"Drummond, I want you to look into where the letters were posted. The first three – and Marlowe said his also – were all posted at the same time in Arnos Grove. However, I'll be surprised if our writer lives anywhere near there. I've made enquiries, and it seems the letter box is within fifty yards of Arnos Grove station. We know the collection was at seven in the morning, but when you go to the box check when the last collection was the previous evening. That'll give us the range of times between which the letters were posted.

"Ask staff at the station. Someone might remember seeing an individual alight from a train – from either direction – who then came back to the station minutes later and got on another train. A long shot, but we have to start somewhere. And if that individual was carrying pale blue envelopes, so much the better. That's an even longer shot, but we can always hope.

"If you get no joy at the station, spend a bit of time asking at properties close to the letter box. That's an even longer shot, but every day there are plenty of examples up and down the country of police being helped by the most casual of bystanders, and in the most unexpected of ways.

"Take the underground to Arnos Grove. On the way back, get out at King's Cross – aim to be there at two forty-five. I'll pick you up in front of the station, and the two of us will go and visit Dr Marlowe."

Bryce was about to move on when he changed his mind and addressed Drummond again. "Have you been to that station before?"

Drummond said that that he hadn't.

"Well, it's arguably the best on the London Underground, Constable, and I rank its architect, Charles Holden, one of the greatest in his profession. Unlike Lutyens, also one of my heroes, Holden actually declined the offer of a knighthood – twice, in fact. Since he's still with us and Lutyens isn't, that makes him the finest living British architect, in my view. You can count yourself lucky you're being paid to spend even a few minutes at Arnos Grove."

Drummond, who knew nothing of architecture or architects and was still counting himself lucky to work with a Chief Superintendent who actually deigned to shake his hand, gave the standard response of 'Sir!' and determined to take note of the station.

Bryce gave his next instructions to Inspector Haig. "I want you to see DI Haynes at Putney. Collect the letter he's holding. Go through the farce of trying for prints, of course.

Bring back whatever evidence Haynes may have to suggest that the valet is, or isn't, our man. Then go and interview Galbraith and see what you can get from him. You aren't interested in the murder – just the blackmail.

"Finally you, Kittow. You're a Kentish Man – so obviously our best candidate for a trip out to the High Weald. Easiest to take a train, but make contact with Tonbridge before you go, and arrange for someone to take you to Barratt's house. Collect Barratt's letter, and bring it back here for tests. Go through his papers thoroughly – at his office too, if he has one. Follow up anything worthwhile that occurs to you whilst you're there.

"That leaves me to see the Bishop this morning.

"If you have anything urgent to report, call in and leave a message with my Secretary. Provisionally, let's try to meet back here at about half past four – but don't drop something important just to make that time.

"Everyone clear on what you have to do?"

The three detectives nodded.

CHAPTER 7

Bryce contemplated either walking to the Goring or taking the underground to Victoria, before deciding to take a bus. Climbing the stairs to the top deck, and seeing an unoccupied pair of seats in the front window, he settled himself to take in the finest moving panorama of the city which he so loved. Getting off at Grosvenor Gardens, he walked the few yards to Beeston Place.

Quick strides took him up the steps to the hotel's entrance, where he was greeted by a commissionaire, even more elegantly attired, if that were possible, than the corresponding man at the Savoy. At the reception desk, he identified himself as Mr Wilson, and asked for the Prelate.

"His lordship informed me that he was expecting a visitor, sir. The boy will show you up."

With a snap of the fingers a uniformed page, young enough to be barely out of school and short trousers, appeared. Bryce followed his escort until the lad stopped and knocked on a second-floor door.

The door had hardly opened an inch before the youngster shot off again, so abruptly that Bryce couldn't proffer the tip he was fishing for.

"Come in, my dear chap," said the bishop in a fruity baritone. Formally dressed in a purple shirt, short cassock, breeches, and gaiters, Bryce wasn't at all surprised to see the silk top hat, which would complete the prelate's formal outfit, sitting on a side table.

With the civilities of introduction and a question about refreshments dealt with, Bryce took the seat indicated and turned the conversation to matters of substance.

"I've read the letter you received, Bishop, but I do need to know of anything you can tell me about possible authors."

Charrington sighed. "I really have no idea. None at all. I've racked my brains ever since it arrived, but nothing comes to me. And as the allegations are totally unfounded, I suppose the letter could have been written by someone who doesn't know me at all and has just made up a story – perhaps some fanatical anti-cleric."

"Have you mentioned this to anyone else, Bishop?"

"Not a soul. I was so horrified I almost destroyed the contemptible thing. My Chaplain normally opens my incoming post, but it happened that he was sick that morning. Although, once he saw the *'Strictly Personal'* heading on the envelope, he probably wouldn't have opened it. I have no way of telling, because I don't recall ever receiving an item of correspondence addressed like that."

"Have you noticed the sentences about *'unpleasant revelations'*, and the mention of *'two instances'*?"

"I saw them, of course. Do you think they're significant?"

"Perhaps. You aren't the only person to receive a letter of this sort in the last couple of days, Bishop. We know of five others. All are from Nemesis, only differing in the allegations and the sums demanded. The ones we've seen so far all contain what I think is a hint that there could be further allegations – and further demands."

The Bishop looked very unhappy at this.

Bryce continued. "The other recipients include at least two people that you know – Lord Hartley, and David Poole."

"Great Scott!" exclaimed the Bishop. "I'm slightly acquainted with both men, although I've never had much contact with either. I hardly dare ask what is alleged about them, and I doubt you would tell me?"

"No, but like you, each insists that there is nothing unlawful in the allegations made in his letter.

"Other recipients are Stuart Galbraith, Simon Marlowe, and Julian Barratt."

The Bishop shook his head. "I don't remember hearing any of those names before.

But it must be a good sign that all these people decided to stand up to this blackmailer, and report the matter to the police?"

"Up to a point, yes. However, they didn't all make a report. Mr Barratt committed suicide yesterday; his letter was found with his body.

"As for Mr Galbraith, he apparently formed the view that he knew the blackmailer and shot his suspect dead. Whether or not he got the right man, he carried out a punishment that went completely beyond what would have been delivered in court."

The Bishop sat staring at Bryce in horror. "The letters are surely all the work of a madman, trying to bring down prominent men by maliciously sullying them!"

"Possibly. But it has to be accepted that the blackmailer has some knowledge of each of you. Mr Poole and Lord Hartley don't deny the facts, but claim that what was alleged wasn't unlawful. I haven't spoken to any other recipients yet.

"I'm accusing you of nothing, Bishop, but you do need to think who might have some reason to suspect that you did what is stated. This business of appointing someone to a living, for instance."

"It's rubbish, Chief Superintendent, complete rubbish! The blackmailer doesn't even give a name. I would never take a bribe in exchange for a living – it's unthinkable.

"As for the plate, yes, I did sell three

pieces, so that much is true. But they weren't exceptional or particularly valuable items of Church silver, and they hadn't been used at Communion in living memory. As the incumbent, I considered I had every right to dispose of them and put the proceeds towards the upkeep of the church – money which was sorely needed at the time."

"Can you think of someone who would have been aware of that incident, and who would also have been privy to any appointments you made later, when elevated to the bishopric?"

"I can't."

"Well, please give it careful thought," said Bryce. "The incident in Dorset, for example. Make a list of every single person who was aware of your action; members of the Parochial Church Council and churchwardens or sidesmen for a start. Your curate if you had one, and any staff who might have overheard discussions. You should include the dealer or auctioneer who handled the sale, and the buyer, too, if you know who that was. Let me have your list as a matter of urgency.

"Finally, I see it as inevitable that you'll get a further communication, as there's no indication in this first round of letters how the author expects his victims to pay. Please let me know immediately you hear anything."

Bryce stood up and extended his hand. "I hope this unpleasantness doesn't spoil your lunch, Bishop."

***

Detective Constable Drummond was always happy to take the underground for short journeys, but today wished he'd been able to take a car instead. Just to get onto the Piccadilly Line from Westminster meant two changes of train. Because the day was fine he decided to walk up to Piccadilly Circus instead, from where he could take a direct, fourteen-stop tube train. Although a Londoner through and through, he realised that he had never travelled on this line beyond King's Cross.

At Arnos Grove, the train emerged above ground for the first time and Drummond alighted. Hanging back until the other passengers dispersed, he quickly spotted the platform official. He waited until the train had been waved off before approaching to explain what he was after.

Up close, the detective saw that the man's London Transport uniform was the one thing which saved him from resembling an old derelict. In his sixties, with a lined and grizzled face, his thin grey hair was straggling out untidily from under his uniform hat. The remaining teeth which he showed in his smile were either rotten or thickly coated with tobacco stains.

As unprepossessing as he was, Basil Eccles

was helpful in his responses to Drummond's questions. "Yeah," he agreed, "I worked that evenin' shift. My job's to signal trains away from the platform when all's clear. An' there was a geezer who come and went within a few minutes. 'Bout 'alf past nine. Didn't really look that closely when 'e arrived on the Eastbound, but you'd be surprised how many people you manage to notice wivout even tryin' in a job like this. I find it 'elps break up the workin' day to observe me fellow-man a bit; an' me fellow-woman too!" he said with a leery wink.

"Few minutes later, blow me down if I don't see 'im again, standin' on the platform waitin' for a Westbound train. Only 'alf a dozen passengers on that side at the time. 'E weren't unusual in any way – medium height, glasses, dark overcoat wiv a scarf, an' a trilby on his loaf. But dressed like a businessman an' not a labourer nor anyone 'oo does 'ard graft, that's for sure."

Eccles gave Drummond time to note all this down.

"No question it was the same man both times. I thought 'e was someone come to look at the station – we do get 'em – but they tend to visit in daylight. Mind you, no act of parleymint says they can't have a quick gander later in the day though, is there?" he asked rhetorically. "But, if 'e come to look 'e didn't spend much time doin' it, is all I'd say. Thought it a bit odd at the time."

"About how old would he be?" asked the

detective.

Air was slowly sucked through the remaining teeth. "Between thirty and forty, p'raps, but I couldn't swear to that." Eccles bared his yellowing and decaying stumps in another smile. "Ages are 'ard to guess – 'oo'd think I'm as old as forty-four to look at me, eh?"

Drummond thought absolutely no one would think the London Transport man was anywhere near as *young* as forty-four, and wondered if Eccles was joking, but didn't laugh in case the man was serious. He put another question.

"Can you remember if he was carrying anything?"

"Yeah; black briefcase. Tha's another thing which sort of stood out – not many business people go back to the City at that time o' night."

"Very useful," said Drummond. Pleased with the information he'd been given so far, he felt that Basil Eccles was a reliable witness. With heightened hopes he asked, "Might you recognise him, if you saw him again?"

Air was now slowly expelled through the neglected teeth. "If I see 'im on the platforms again – in 'is original settin' so to speak, an' movin' about naturally in the same sort o' clothes, then yeah, I reckon I could pick 'im out pretty quick. Bit different just standin' like a statue in a line-up though – might not be quite so sure about it there. But glad to give it a try, if it 'elps."

"Thanks a lot, Mr Eccles. If you do see him again, ring the Yard straight away, please." Drummond wrote the necessary information on the last sheet of his pocketbook and tore it out.

"Will do," agreed the guard amiably, accepting the page and folding it carefully before slipping it into his uniform breast pocket. "Every shift I'm 'ere, this'll be 'ere wiv me," he said, giving the pocket a double tap with his hand. But do I need to be worried if I see 'im again? Wot's 'e done?"

Drummond wasn't quite sure how to answer this, as the mysterious passenger might be a perfectly innocent citizen. On the other hand, he didn't want to minimise the importance of this sighting. He came up with a compromise.

"We're investigating a very nasty business, Mr Eccles. This man may or may not have anything to do with it. But there's no violence involved, I assure you."

"Ah, good. I wouldn't want any more of me teeth knocked out in a round of fisticuffs wiv yer man! If you go up the top, Freddie Laws in the passimeter was on that evening. I don't know if the bloke bought a ticket comin' back, but Freddie might remember 'im."

Taking the escalator to the circular booking hall, Drummond paused to look around, and tried unsuccessfully to work out why the

Chief Superintendent had thought so highly of the station. He could see it was unusual, but the young officer had never really thought much about architecture and design before. If a building did its job, that was enough for him. Still, from what Eccles had said others seemed to find something to admire, and whilst he waited for an opportunity to speak to the clerk he made a renewed effort to note distinctive features, in case the Chief Super quizzed him later.

As soon as the queue at the booking window cleared, the Constable went to speak to Freddie Laws. He explained his task, and that Basil Eccles had sent him up.

"I was here, all right," agreed Laws. "There's not that many people buying tickets that time of night. I did notice a man inning and outing; but people do that sometimes y'know, all absent minded. Got out at the wrong station, maybe. The old 'uns are the worst for it, but they usually realise as soon as they're in the street; I've watched them turn around and come straight back inside again many a time.

"Your man was different, and that's partly why I remember him. He completely left the building and was gone a few minutes. Then he came back. He obviously had the right money because he got himself a ticket," Laws pointed to the wall opposite where some experimental self-service ticket machines had recently been installed. "No idea what fare he bought, though."

Drummond asked for a description, and found himself recording most of the same points that Eccles had mentioned.

"Would you recognise him again?"

Laws considered. "Not sure about that. He was what I'd call a 'type' if y'know what I mean. Lots of blokes look like him and dress like him. Walk and talk like him, too, probably – not that I heard him speak."

Laws was as willing as his colleague to help in any way he could, but the corners of his mouth drooped and he shook his head. "Hand on heart, doubt I could recognise him good enough to swear to it. Leastways, not unless you've already nabbed your villain and I can see him before what's in my memory fades?"

The corners of Drummond's mouth now also drooped. "We're not that close yet, unfortunately," he said. Thanking Laws for his help, he repeated his request to ring the Yard immediately if the man should appear again, and provided another sheet from his pocketbook with contact details.

Believing that he had sufficient confirmation that the Chief Super's theory was probably correct, and armed with at least a vague description, he decided against knocking on doors and instead went to find the pillar box. As predicted, it was within fifty yards of the station entrance. The unknown man could certainly have been out of the station and back again in very few minutes. The DC noted that the previous collection would have been at six o' clock on the Monday evening. Eccles' sighting at half-past nine was certainly consistent with someone visiting the station to post the blackmail letters in the nearby box.

Satisfied that he had something to report, Drummond took the train back to King's Cross, where he bought and quickly downed a sandwich and a cup of coffee, before waiting for his boss outside the station.

CHAPTER 8

Inspector Haig also travelled by underground train, in his case to Putney Bridge. It was a short walk from there to the police station. He had never come across DI Ronald Haynes before, and found him to be a cheerful man of about his own age.

"Let's have a cup of tea in my office, while we talk about all this," said Haynes. He instructed a constable to produce a brew. "Decent stuff please, Nunn, not the usual sweepings." Haig was escorted to a very small office on the first floor.

Within minutes, the two men were on first-name terms, and laughing over various work experiences. With their beverages served, they got down to business.

"Bit of a shock for me, Alex, having the Assistant Commissioner on the blower explaining your blackmail case." He handed his Yard counterpart a folder. "Here's the infamous letter for you by the way, and the envelope it arrived in. No prints on the letter apart from

Galbraith's."

Haig set the folder aside for the moment as he listened to Haynes.

"When our uniformed chaps turned up in response to a neighbour's report of two gunshots, Galbraith opened the door straight away, no fuss. Our men could smell the cordite, so they knew it was the right flat.

"Galbraith was co-operative throughout; admitted he'd shot his valet and took our boys into the living room. Crossland was on the floor, face up. Yellow duster in hand."

Haig's head shot back at this, his dark eyebrows disappearing into his hairline as he snorted loudly.

"I know, I know!" said Haynes, holding up his hands and shaking his head. "Galbraith's excuse was: 'he came for me so I had to shoot him'. Alarm bells immediately rang for our men at that gem!"

"Aye," said Haig. "Not many people walk about carrying a loaded automatic indoors on the off chance a servant will jump out at them with a duster. And most people armed with only a duster, have the sense not to jump out at someone holding a pistol!"

Haynes grinned. "Too right. He was arrested on suspicion there and then, and brought here.

"I spoke to him in the cells as soon as he arrived. He turned down having a solicitor. That was when he first mentioned the valet trying to blackmail him, and the letter.

"I rounded up my Sergeant and the Police Surgeon and went to the flat. Took no time for our Doc to confirm there were two shots fired – and wait for this, Alex – from a distance of at least twelve feet."

Haig snorted again. "That certainly puts the tin lid on Galbraith claiming he was attacked by Crossland – or that the two of them were having a struggle at the time."

Haynes nodded. "We found the blackmail letter lying open on Galbraith's desk in his study, with absolutely nothing else of interest that we could see. So we rooted around in the valet's room with a view to finding anything to corroborate what Galbraith said about Crossland being the blackmailer.

"Nothing at all to positively make that link for you, Alex, but..." Haynes produced another file and opened it for the Yard Inspector, "what we did find was this part-written letter. Probably to his sister, judging by the way he enquires after her husband, and further down calls him 'brother-in-law'."

Haynes indicated there was another sheet beneath Crossland's letter. "He'd also written a list of the duties Galbraith had set him for certain days of the week; we found it pinned to the back of his door. Easy work to match the handwriting on the list with the letter to his sister, and conclude they've been written by the same person."

"And even easier," said Haig as he studied the two examples, "to conclude that Crossland was only semi-literate. His letter has an error on every line, and even the list has spelling mistakes."

Haig closed the folder. "My opinion is that our blackmailer isn't in your morgue with a name tag tied to his toe."

"Yep, that's how I see it as well."

"By the way, the murder aspect of all this is yours, Ron," added Haig. "We're only interested in the blackmail."

"More than happy to take that on," said the local DI, with an expression on his face that fully matched his words. "At least I don't have to look very far to find my killer!"

Haynes pointed to the first folder. "How many of these blackmail letters are there?"

"Six that we know of," Haig told him, "but not all of them in our possession yet. Three addressed to people so prominent that they got access to the Commissioner personally. Those three are all a bit odd, because the accusations may not be criminal at all."

"Definitely a criminal matter in that one," said Haynes, pointing to Galbraith's blackmail letter folder again, "and with added social stigma for him."

Haig nodded. "Give me a minute to look

at it, and I'll tell you how it compares with the others I've seen." Haig opened the folder and read the letter twice before giving his assessment.

"From *'Nemesis'*, and some identical phrasing to the others I've seen, just a different allegation. And as you say, a criminal matter this time." Haig glanced at the letter again. "Galbraith is expected to cough up a thousand pounds. Is he rich?"

Haynes gave a rumbling laugh. "Ha! To me, anyone who keeps a valet is rich. He was a private banker at one of the largest international firms, the sort that stays behind the scenes and moves big money in and out of commercial enterprises. Beautiful flat – the grandest I've ever been in, and he drives a Bentley. So yes, he's prosperous all right, which is just as well, because he'll need well-filled pockets to pay counsel to come up with any sort of defence for what he's done."

The local DI picked up his internal telephone and asked for Galbraith to be taken to an interview room. "Let's go and talk to him when we've finished our tea," he suggested.

Their mugs drained, the two DIs went downstairs and joined the retired banker in the small and secure room where he sat waiting with a watchful constable.

"Good morning, Mr Galbraith," said Haynes cordially. "This is Inspector Haig from Scotland Yard. He's interested in the blackmail letter you received. Before we start, I'll remind you that you remain under the caution you were given yesterday. If you want to change your mind about a solicitor, you can say at any time."

Appraising the prisoner as Haynes spoke, Haig felt a degree of pity for the anxious and crushed-looking man on the other side of the table. Perhaps sixty-five years of age, he was dressed in the purple satin quilted smoking jacket he had been wearing when arrested. The fabric, trimmed with thick cords of gold braid, gleamed under the electric light in the windowless room.

Haig, ready to start his enquiry, thought Galbraith couldn't have looked more out of place – or less like a criminal. "Yours is the sixth similar letter that's come to our attention in the last forty-eight hours, Mr Galbraith," he said. "The only differences are in the allegations made, and in the amount the author expects his victims to pay.

"This 'Nemesis' knows, or says he knows, something about all of you – so there must be a connection between you. Obviously, that's what we're looking for. Do you know any of the following people: David Poole, the MP; Caspar Charrington, the Bishop of Crewe; Lord Peregrine Hartley; Julian Barratt; Simon Marlowe?"

Galbraith, slumped dejectedly in his seat when the DIs arrived, now straightened up, his manner and posture instantly transformed to alertness. "These people receiving letters like mine surely shines a different light on things, doesn't it, Inspector? Are they all successful and prosperous men that some criminal lowlife wants to utterly destroy?

"As for your question, I've heard of Poole, of course, and of Lord Hartley. I'm also aware there is a Bishop of Crewe. To my knowledge I've never met any of them. The names of the last two...no, I don't believe I've even heard of them."

"Apart from your valet, do you employ anyone else?"

"Not any more. I live in a serviced flat now. Crossland did some superficial housekeeping for me, but I have meals sent in as required, and everything else – laundry and more thorough cleaning – is carried out by the flat management company. I used to have a large house. Until about a year ago when I retired from banking and sold up, I employed six domestic staff and a gardener."

Haig now began the sequence of questions which he hoped might open up the investigation. "Mr Galbraith, we make no moral judgement about the allegations in the letter, and neither of us is interested in following up any alleged offence in that regard. But you should know that the various accusations levelled at other recipients are based on fact. That being so, would you like to comment on the allegation levelled at you?"

Galbraith was at once dejected again.

When he next spoke he did so quietly. "It's true that my intimate preferences don't extend to women; they never have. But I've always been discreet, and those I've associated with have been equally discreet."

"Can you think of anyone, other than your valet, who might have known or suspected?"

"The absence of a wife or female visitors to my home would probably lead some to the correct conclusion. I'll give you a list of servants' names if that will help."

Haynes passed him a sheet of paper and a pen. Galbraith wrote, then pushed the paper towards the Yard detective.

Haig pushed it straight back at him. "What names can you supply in addition to former staff?" he asked.

Galbraith bristled. For a moment it looked as though he wouldn't answer, before changing his mind and stating, "I've worked for the same merchant bank since the Great War, but I'd be utterly astounded if many people there had the slightest inkling of my preferences. I kept a picture of my late sister on my desk; she died in 1917 after a Zeppelin raid. I didn't correct people who thought she was a lost sweetheart and the reason why I never married."

The retired banker was on the verge of becoming angry now, and almost shouted at Haig and Haynes.

"I refuse to name the few of my old

colleagues whom I know shared my inclinations – ones whom I'd met by accident in the very private clubs which cater for like-minded men. I never mixed my business life with my private life and I simply cannot believe that any of them would betray me in this way. Quite apart from the serious risk of blackmail, they would never risk their own positions!"

Haig, whilst understanding Galbraith's reluctance to involve anyone else, felt confused about what he had been told. He sought clarification. "You've just offered up – without hesitation or quibble – the names of six long-standing employees from your former home who might have been involved in blackmailing you. Why on earth did you suddenly pick on Crossland alone as the author?"

Galbraith's voice returned to normal and he responded decisively to the question. "It had to be him; I've had servants for decades and no blackmail attempt. Not one. I engage him and two months later the letter arrives!"

Haig persisted. "But could he even have found anything out in that time?"

"When I was still working there was always considerable pressure to ensure I did nothing which might jeopardise my employment or bring the bank into disrepute. I became rather more relaxed about the security of my private life after I retired." The look of regret on Galbraith's face was almost painful to witness. "I think it wouldn't have been difficult for Crossland to guess," he concluded.

Haynes took over the questioning.

"We've looked closely at the blackmail letter sent to you, Mr Galbraith. Do you agree with us that it wasn't composed by an illiterate person?"

The retired banker looked very unhappy indeed as he acknowledged this fact with a half-hearted nod.

"And yet, from what evidence we can find of your late valet's penmanship, his written English was poor. And no typewriter was found in his room. So I'll repeat Inspector Haig's question in a different way. How could you possibly think it was Crossland?"

"Frankly, I didn't think about the writing at the time. But if I had thought more – as I've had time to do overnight in your cell – I'd have assumed that he sold the information to a better-educated person. Which amounts to the same thing for me. Crossland was my blackmailer."

This was an answer that at least made sense.

Haig had another question. "Back to yesterday. When you accused Crossland of attempted blackmail, did he deny it?"

"Yes, immediately. Then he just came at me."

With this statement of Crossland's denial, Haig knew there was nothing more for him to learn regarding the blackmail element of the confrontation in Galbraith's flat. The fact that the valet's denial might have been a worthless lie didn't help him from an investigation point of view, because the denial left him no lead to follow.

Had Crossland admitted to his master that he was involved, Haig was quite sure Galbraith would have successfully extracted more information from the valet at the point of his automatic. Alternatively, Galbraith could have held Crossland captive at gunpoint and called the police to question him. Exactly as in Barratt's case, premature death had extinguished any chance of making further enquiries.

Haig had no choice but to accept this sterile end to his questioning. He sat back and observed as Inspector Haynes finished the interview by giving Galbraith the Police Surgeon's opinion of the twelve-foot distance at which he had shot his valet.

Galbraith had only one response. "I want to speak to my solicitor. Michael Head, of Poulter, Pearson and Head, if you please."

Haynes nodded, and shouted for someone to take Galbraith back to the cells and then to make the arrangements for the solicitor.

With the prisoner removed, Haig stood and tucked his chair under the table. "I'd like to go through Galbraith's papers at the flat now, and take a look in Crossland's room, if you've no objection?"

"Nope; I need to look round again as well. We can go straight there."

The flat was only a short car ride away. On arrival, Haynes made a drawing of the layout of the room and then went to interview some neighbours, while Haig spent half an hour going through the retired banker's desk and files.

"Nothing much of interest," he reported when the local DI returned. "But I'll take his address book, which may help us. I doubt if you'll need it for your case, but say if you do and I'll make sure you get it back.

"By the way," Haig handed over a folded paper to his counterpart. "Galbraith's firearms certificate. A minor point in the scheme of things, but his automatic is held legally. I know from police training that it isn't easy to shoot accurately with a pistol, even at such short range. I'll bet ten bob that you find he not only served in the first war, but was probably a good shot."

"I'm not taking that bet," laughed Haynes.

CHAPTER 9

Detective Constable Kittow walked to Charing Cross station. From there he took a train to Tonbridge, where he was met by Detective Sergeant Bailey.

As he climbed into the unmarked police car, Kittow thought Bailey looked a bored and cynical sort of individual. During the journey to Barratt's house he had no reason to alter this first impression.

"Obviously bent, was Barratt," opined the Sergeant as he drove. "Topping himself was probably the best thing he ever did.

"And this Hartley bloke that's mentioned in Barratt's letter; he'll be guilty too."

"Hartley's had a blackmail letter himself, Sarge," replied Kittow.

Bailey grinned from ear to ear and banged the rim of the steering wheel with his fist. "There you are then! Just as I said.

"I've got Barratt's letter nice and snug in that folder on the back seat for you, but I'm told you want to search through the rest of his papers." Bailey managed to imply, sarcastically, that his time was being wasted.

"That's right, the Chief Super wants me to look. Although as he said, it would've been better if we could have talked to Barratt," added Kittow, by way of making conversation.

Another spiteful grin spread across Bailey's face. "Want me to take you to the morgue then, so you can talk to him there? I think he'll exercise his right to remain silent, though!" He guffawed and banged the steering wheel again.

Kittow didn't find his companion's humour or manner engaging, and he didn't speak again for the rest of the journey.

Barratt's residence was large and detached, in a broad tree-lined avenue. Bailey had brought the house keys and let them in, bending to pick up the newspaper on the mat as he did so.

"Do we know where the ex-wife is, Sarge?" asked Kittow, before moving towards the room which Bailey pointed out as the study.

"Yes, lad. We asked the neighbours yesterday, and they reckoned they hadn't seen her in over a year. But we found her details in the address book on the desk; she's somewhere in Lytham St Annes. The Lancashire boys are looking for her today. You can help yourself to the book – we're done with it."

Bailey waved dismissively at Kittow. Instead of accompanying and assisting the Yard detective, he walked further down the hallway, opened the living room door and settled himself into an armchair. "And there's the name of a solicitor, too," he shouted to the now out-of-sight DC. "We figured you'd be more interested in him than we are, so he's all yours – we've not spoken to him. Man called Gibbs."

Kittow turned back and went to stand in the living room doorway. "Did Barratt have an office anywhere?"

Bailey yawned. "No. One of the neighbours said he used to have an office, but for at least a year now he's done all his shady business from home."

Sarcasm returned to the Sergeant's voice as he shook out the newspaper. "Need me to hold your hand for you any more, Constable? Or can you manage to do your job like a big boy now, and leave me in peace?"

Kittow was fulminating as he left the room, but quietly went to work in his usual professional manner. In the study he methodically searched Barratt's desk and filing cabinets, but saw nothing which was likely to help the investigation. He slipped the address book into his pocket, first recording the name and address of the solicitor in his own notebook.

As the detectives left the house, Bailey suddenly deigned to share something else. "The inquest," he said, "someone'll have to give evidence about the letter. Better get your boss to talk to mine about how that ceremony should be played."

Kittow acknowledged this. Asking to be dropped off at the solicitor's office, the Yard detective sat in silence for the journey. When the car pulled up outside Gibbs' premises, he took the folder holding Barratt's blackmail letter from the back seat. As he climbed out of the car, he tossed an off-hand 'goodbye' towards Bailey and didn't bother to thank the lazy and unpleasant Sergeant before he slammed the car door shut.

Standing on the pavement, Kittow could see that the solicitor's office was small, and from the sign outside he deduced that it was a singleton practice. Inside, he found a slightly built girl of about twenty, bashing away at a typewriter with a force and speed which belied her stature. She paused to look up at him.

Nice-looking, he thought. Not a beauty, but somehow striking. He introduced himself, showed his warrant card, and explained that he needed to speak to Mr Gibbs personally about a client named Julian Barratt.

The girl was concerned. "Oh yes," she said, "I know Mr Barratt. I do hope this doesn't mean there's trouble for him with the police."

Kittow registered this as genuine hope on the girl's part, as she made no attempt to fish for details.

"Mr Gibbs is out of the office just now," she said, "he's gone for a bite to eat. He'll be back in ten or fifteen minutes, though, and his next appointment isn't until half past three. If you want to wait, I can easily rustle up a cup of something for you."

"That's very kind, Miss, but I think I'll find something to eat myself. Will you tell Mr Gibbs I'll come back at half past one? It's a very important matter."

A smile and rapid nods confirmed that his message would be passed on.

As he turned towards the door Kittow looked back and asked the helpful girl, "Where's nice to eat that's nearby, Miss? Just for something quick and simple."

He found the recommended tea shop in the next street and enjoyed a warm Cornish pasty with a cup of coffee, before returning to the office at the promised time.

The receptionist got up as soon as he walked through the front door, and smilingly led him to another door. She tapped on this and immediately pushed it open.

"Detective Constable Kittow for you, Mr Gibbs," she announced.

"Come right in, officer, and take a seat." The solicitor, a man in his late thirties with a far more pleasant manner than Sergeant Bailey's, shook Kittow's hand.

"Jilly tells me you want to talk about Julian Barratt. I'm intrigued as to why the police are interested in him. However, I hope first of all that he isn't in trouble, and second that you aren't going to try to get me to reveal privileged information!"

Kittow hesitated. "Well, sir, in one sense he is in trouble; and in another he isn't. I'll fill you in. He received a letter – a blackmail threat alleging corrupt practices in his business affairs. The demand payable for silence was a thousand pounds."

Gibbs looked slightly lost. "Very sensible of him to report this to the police. Exactly what I would have suggested if he'd asked me for advice." He shook his head. "But he didn't."

"He didn't come to us either, sir," Kittow told him. "We don't know whether or not he even thought about coming doing so. All we know is that the letter warned him not to approach the police – and that he shot himself. The blackmail letter was found with him. There was no suicide note, but perhaps Mr Barratt thought the letter was self-explanatory."

The solicitor was now gaping at Kittow. Pushing his spectacles back to the bridge of his nose, he exclaimed, "Oh dear Lord! What a frightful mess. But hang on. Jilly saw your warrant card – she says you're from the Metropolitan Police, not the local constabulary. What's going on? And how do you think I can help?"

"Observant girl, sir. Yes, I'm from Scotland Yard.

"There's been a number of almost identical

letters in the last couple of days. We know of five more, and all those were sent to men in London, or with strong London connections. Mr Barratt is the only provincial one we've come across."

"Some of the letters have been addressed to very prominent people; members of the Commons and the Lords, for a start. Detective Chief Superintendent Bryce is leading the investigation.

"As to how you could help, were you privy to any transactions of Mr Barratt's which might shed some light on all this? Perhaps you were involved in drawing up his business contracts?"

Gibbs' voice was now confident as he replied. "In drawing them up, never. Quite often, though, Julian would ask me to look at a particular clause in a contract or some other document, and advise him as to what it meant in layman's terms. I found him surprisingly naïve about what I should have thought were everyday business expressions; so much so that I always assumed that most of his dealings were oral. Indeed, I heard him say more than once that a handshake was as good as a written contract any day. I remember trying to suggest that he was wrong, but he just laughed. The contracts he showed me were ones which another party wanted; I don't think he ever initiated any written ones himself – certainly not through me.

"I did draw up his will a few years ago – all very straightforward. His ex-wife and adult children share the estate. I'm the executor."

Kittow first emphasised that the information he was about to share was confidential, but given that Gibbs was an officer of the court he had no hesitation in revealing the names of the other blackmail victims.

"If I tell you that each of the letters implies that more wrong doing might be revealed, would you happen to know what Mr Barratt feared?" asked the detective. "Because at the moment we're in the dark as to whether it was the accusation in his letter, or the threat of something worse to follow that caused him to take his own life."

Gibbs slowly moved his head from side to side. "No, not a clue, I'm afraid."

"Lord Hartley. I assume you've heard of him?"

"Of course. Who hasn't? He seems to own half the country if you can believe what the papers say about his acquisitions."

"The thing is, sir, the allegation against Mr Barratt is that he conspired with his lordship to defraud some person or company."

Gibbs again stared at Kittow for some seconds, looking shocked.

"I had no idea that Julian knew Hartley – if in fact he did. I'll do anything I can to help, but I say again, I wasn't involved in drawing up any of his contracts and so on. I always assumed from his lifestyle that he was successful in whatever he did. We're both members of the same golf club, Rotary, and so on. He was a fairly prominent person around here, but not, I should have thought, in the habit of hobnobbing with peers or MPs. We don't have any of those in the golf club!"

"Just one last point, sir. We've found Mr Barratt's address book. It may be that my Chief Superintendent would like to ask if you know any of the people listed in it. But that'll wait until we've sifted through it ourselves and seen if any of the names tie in with our other enquiries."

Gibbs nodded his understanding and Kittow stood up to leave.

"Thank you again for your time, sir," said the detective, and saw himself out of the solicitor's office.

Keen to be able to show his boss that he was efficient as well as trustworthy – unlike his ex-colleague Yapp – Kittow spent the journey time back to Charing Cross conscientiously reviewing his actions. It didn't occur to him that he would never have been given such an important task if the DCS hadn't already thought him capable.

CHAPTER 10

Many people were milling around outside King's Cross station when Drummond emerged from the underground. After a moment's indecision, he went to stand almost on the corner of Pancras Road, directly opposite the clock tower end of what had once been the Midland Grand hotel. He knew that the Chief Superintendent was coming from Belgravia, and that they would be going out again from the station in the same direction from which he had come. He thought it was pretty certain that the Chief would turn in to Pancras Road rather than making a U-turn in the main road.

He was correct; within a couple of minutes a big Wolseley swept round the corner, turned in front of the Great Northern Hotel, and came to a halt beside the Constable. Drummond climbed self-consciously into the front passenger seat and Bryce eased the car forward. Spotting a gap in the traffic he pulled across both carriageways before accelerating westwards along the Euston Road.

"Any success, Drummond?" he asked.

"Up to a point, sir. Just as you thought, there was a man who arrived at the station, somewhere around nine-thirty that evening – and who came back a few minutes later and took another train in the direction he'd come. I confirmed that the pillar box is about fifty yards from the station entrance. The previous collection was at six o'clock.

"The two London Transport men I spoke to gave descriptions which tally, but they're not much help, sir. Not old. Dark overcoat: navy or black. Scarf. Spectacles. Trilby. Brief case. Half the men in London – maybe England – who fit the age range might fit the rest of the descriptions.

"Only thing is, sir, the employee on the platform reckons he might recognise the man again. So if you get a suspect, we could try an identification parade."

Bryce was pleased. "Well done, Drummond. That does seem to confirm my theory, and it almost certainly means that our author doesn't live around Arnos Grove.

"But it doesn't get us much further unless, as you say, we find someone to parade in front of the underground man.

"Now, what did you think of the station?"

Drummond turned sideways to look at his boss, but Bryce's eyes were fixed on the road ahead.

"Unusual, I suppose, sir," began the young

detective, realising as soon as he spoke that he had already run out of things to say.

"Oh dear me," said the Chief Superintendent. "I fear you're one of those who doesn't appreciate architecture. A terrible thing, with all the varied buildings, monuments, and so on in London. Hitler managed to destroy a lot, of course, but what remains is as good a collection as you'll find anywhere in the world.

"Within sight of where you were standing just now, for example, are at least three buildings of note. King's Cross station and its associated hotel were built for the Great Northern Railway in the 1850s, both designed by Lewis Cubitt. Then in the 1860s the Midland Railway decided it needed to extend into London – partly because the Great Northern charged a high toll on carrying coal and so on into the city.

"So they built St Pancras – a wonder of its time, as its train shed with a single-span roof became the largest enclosed space in the world for a while. In front of the station they built the Midland Grand hotel, designed in high Victorian Gothic by Sir Gilbert Scott. Rumour has it that when entering the competition to design the hotel he completely ignored the specification – his offering was larger and far more expensive. However, his design won, although the railway directors made him lop off a floor and a few other bits.

"Now," he continued, as he made a right

turn into the Edgware Road, "I'm going to set you a task, to be completed in your own time before we solve this case. No idea how long that'll be; could be months. But you should aim to do this within a week or so.

"Go out on the eastbound Piccadilly line again. There are eight stations after Finsbury Park – the 'extension'. Don't get out at Arnos Grove, but get out at each of the other seven in turn. Spend no more than five minutes at each, looking at the exteriors, the ticket halls, and the access to the platforms. Make some notes. When you've done that, come and find me and talk to me about what you've seen.

"This isn't official business, so don't use your free police pass. When we stop, I'll give you a few pounds to cover the fares, and food and drink for you while on the task.

"Er, right you are then, sir," stammered Drummond. He had vaguely heard that Mr Bryce was very keen on railway systems – and that one of the reasons Mr Haig got on with him so well was that he too was a railway buff. But station architecture, as well? Having been happy to be detailed to work with the Yard's new Inspector and Chief Superintendent, he was beginning to wonder if he would be a good fit.

"I'm not entirely mad," said Bryce with a grin, sensing the young Constable's confusion. "Just looking at something, without really *seeing* it, isn't enough for a detective. You need to develop the art of really seeing – understanding, if you like – what passes in front of your eyes. Those eight stations were all built in the 1930s, when the line was extended to Cockfosters. Each has unique features.

"There's another oddity which you may already know about. Looking at a tube map, and indeed in reality, the extension runs south-north. The last station, Cockfosters, is actually slightly to the west of Oakwood, the previous one, but going in that direction is still called 'eastbound'. The entire Piccadilly line refers to west-east."

The DCS had another thought. "Although I said don't get out again at Arnos Grove, while your train stops there just look at the platform arrangement – not unique but certainly unusual. See if you can appreciate what I mean.

"Now, just get the street map out of the glove box, and find Marlborough Hill. We must be very close."

They turned into the road minutes later, and Bryce pulled up outside one of the area's typical houses – an end property of a three-storey terrace block.

"Your job today is to take notes," instructed Bryce. "Do you have shorthand?"

"Sorry sir; no."

"Never mind. I don't need verbatim details anyway. Just jot down any names and addresses and any crucial points.

"When I've worked with you longer, I'll encourage you to ask your own questions. But until that time comes, if a question occurs to you, write it in your pocketbook and pass it to me.

"Oh, before I forget…" Bryce pulled out his wallet and handed four one-pound notes to the DC. "That should comfortably cover fares and some spending money for two, if you'd like to take a friend with you and make an outing of it."

Drummond looked at the notes and protested. "But that's far too much, sir, even for two!"

The DCS smiled. "I insist," he said. "I'm looking on it as an *ex-gratia* overtime payment that will benefit both me and the force in future, as you develop the skill of 'seeing'."

Finances settled, Bryce locked the car and the officers approached the house, where Bryce pulled on an old iron bell knob. No sound of the bell ringing could be heard by the detectives outside, but after a few seconds a man opened the door.

"Good afternoon; we're here to see Dr Marlowe," said Bryce, without explaining who they were. "He is expecting us."

With the pressure on housing after the war, a property of this size might easily be shared by two or more households. If Dr Marlowe had also received a warning in his letter not to contact the police, no one else answering the door needed to know that the visitors were detectives.

In fact, the man who opened the door immediately introduced himself as the academic they wished to speak to, and the DCS identified himself and his colleague.

"Welcome, gentlemen; please come in," said Marlowe. He turned and led them in single file through a long and narrow hallway, one side of which was crammed with stacked up boxes of books, and a bicycle. An overloaded hallstand, incongruously holding two pairs of antiquated wooden skis in its two umbrella sections, as well as the more usual assortment of apparel on its hooks, covered the last few feet of wall beyond the bicycle. Pushing open a door, the academic led his visitors into a contrastingly neat living room, and invited them to make themselves comfortable in a pair of aged leather armchairs.

Dr Marlowe seated himself opposite, and crossed his legs. The detectives could see he was a good-looking man in his early thirties, clean shaven and with a full head of brown hair. He was dressed in an academic's raiment of leather-patched tweed jacket and slacks, but instead of the more usual checked shirt and plaid woollen tie he wore a high-necked sweater. As the detectives had followed him along the corridor they had both observed that on his feet he had carpet slippers rather than the brogues which might have been expected.

Observing the officers assessing him, and

mistaking their professional interest for some sort of censure, Marlowe smiled engagingly. "This is my day off, and I like to be comfortable around my own home. My attire isn't in any way meant to be insulting to you, my guests. If the Chancellor of my university stepped in for a chat today, my dress would still be the same. Mind you, as he doesn't know I exist, the chance of his arriving is precisely zero!"

He quickly moved on to the reason for the detectives' visit. "You'll want to see why I've contacted the police, of course," he said, and turned to an open bureau. Carefully, he lifted up a rectangle of cardboard. On this were two clean sheets of paper, one had the open letter on top; the other held the envelope. He carried his improvised tray to where Bryce sat, and handed it to him.

"Here's what I received. Obviously, I handled the letter when I opened the envelope, but since then it's been kept as you see it – in case you can get fingerprints."

Bryce read the letter, passing the 'tray' to Drummond when he had finished.

"You told me on the telephone that there's absolutely nothing in these allegations, Dr Marlowe. To your knowledge, has there ever been any previous suggestion that there was?"

The academic's response was firm and final. "None whatsoever. I spent three years working on my doctoral thesis and I can assure you that it was all original work. I'm sure my supervisor, Professor McGrath, will confirm that.

"Eighteen months ago, I published a book. It wasn't hugely well-received in certain quarters because the central premise was fairly revolutionary, and in a few places I flatly contradicted established theories.

"I'll admit that didn't go down well with the people whose work I challenged; and it goes without saying that their adherents were equally put out. And that's what makes this letter so bizarre and inexplicable. I can hardly be accused of plagiarism when I'm smashing down paleontological shibboleths and overturning received wisdoms!"

"Do you know of a particularly unfriendly individual, someone who would go to these extraordinary lengths to discredit you without foundation?"

"No, and that's another reason why I find it all so odd. I have few close friends, none of whom are palaeontology colleagues, and whom I rarely see. In fact, since travel became somewhat easier after the war, I've been able to spend a fair bit of my time fossil hunting overseas – and I make my trips alone.

"When I'm home, I very occasionally meet up with one or two of my old Houghton College rowing pals, and although I have attended one college dinner since I came down I prefer to avoid those. That's about it." The palaeontologist gave a bemused laugh. "Hardly a mad social whirl by today's standards; and certainly not one which puts me in the path of many other people at all – never mind ones who wish to harm me!"

Marlowe shifted in his chair and fixed his gaze intently on Bryce. "I've thought about little else since this arrived, and I've come up with a theory. My name isn't uncommon, and I'd be very surprised if there aren't other Dr Marlowes somewhere – one of whom might have engaged in a bit of plagiarism. There's nothing in the content of the letter, as you see, to tie this to me; in fact it doesn't specify any particular academic discipline. So perhaps this Nemesis got his wires crossed, and this shouldn't have come to me at all?"

"Possible, I suppose," agreed the DCS. "We could try to find one or more others. However, it's probably not worth spending time on that at present, as it's clearly you who'll receive the follow-up letter.

"The thousand pounds demanded; is that within your means?"

Marlowe hesitated. "Probably. I have some private income, and with my work from the Natural History Museum and lecture fees, it's enough to allow me to work on what is really my hobby, and put a bit by for a rainy day, as well.

"But – and I say this without intending an absolute howler of a pun – your question is academic. I haven't the slightest intention of forking over a farthing!"

Bryce asked another question. "Do you think there is an implied threat? That further allegations, beyond plagiarism, could be made?"

Marlowe seized upon this. "Oh! Did you also feel there's a suggestion of more to come? I confess I only picked it up on my third reading, and even then I wasn't quite sure." He shook his head vigorously. "I can tell you without any fear of contradiction that although my life's work is dealing with skeletons in one form or another, I don't actually have any in my own cupboards, gentlemen. I consequently have no fears of any being revealed. As I said, I'm not paying!"

Marlowe's tone left no doubt that he deeply resented the besmirching of his academic efforts and his integrity. Having made his feelings clear, he broached another matter.

"May I change the subject slightly and mention that I'm rather surprised, not to say flattered, to get such a high-ranking officer calling on me? I'd expected a sergeant at best! I only contacted Scotland Yard because I had no idea where to start with making a complaint of this nature; it's hardly in the same league as the time my old bicycle was stolen. So I thought it wouldn't hurt if I started at the top, and that the matter could be passed down to the appropriate level of authority – yet here you are, Chief Superintendent!"

Bryce explained. "If your letter had arrived

a week ago and you'd telephoned the Yard, the case would indeed have been handed over – if not to your local police station, then to your local division to deal with.

"But we know of other letters. A recipient in Kent has killed himself after receiving one. And there have been three very prominent recipients: a cabinet minister; one of the lords spiritual; and one of the lords temporal. It was those three men, all of whom could get the attention of the Chief Commissioner, who explain my involvement."

Marlowe stared at him, flabbergasted. "Five of us? And suggestions about people like peers and Government ministers? I am in exalted company! I take it you're looking for some kind of escaped lunatic?"

"I'm reserving judgement on that," said Bryce, "and it's actually six letters, not five. One recipient has shot the person he suspected of involvement."

Marlowe's face was a picture of shocked horror. "That's simply terrible! You must seize this crazed individual, Chief Superintendent – and quickly!"

"That is our aim, and we have a number of detectives working to that end. You've seen just one letter, but you've no doubt appreciated that, whatever else our correspondent may be, he isn't illiterate. On the contrary, all the letters we've seen are models of how correspondence should be written – apart from the criminal content, of course."

Marlowe apparently hadn't noticed the standard of literacy, and took another look at the letter he had received. "Good heavens, you're right. Hadn't crossed my mind, I must say."

Drummond paused in his notetaking and looked up, his face silently questioning the academic.

"I see you're surprised, officer. But when you're continually immersed as I am – both for work and for pleasure – in exceptionally well-written books and papers, I suppose you only notice the departures," Marlowe told the constable with a friendly smile.

"Speaking of departures," Bryce rose and extended his hand. "Let's see what you and the others receive in the next few days. Please contact me immediately the inevitable follow-up arrives."

"Of course," promised the academic, before guiding them again through the cluttered hallway and to the front door.

CHAPTER 11

"You drive back to the Yard, Drummond. I want to think."

This was only partly true. The Chief Superintendent liked to ascertain the abilities of the officers in his team, and driving skills were included in that assessment. He very soon realised that Drummond knew what he was doing and where he was going. Joining the Edgware Road, the DC drove at a good but not excessive speed to Marble Arch, and then continued down Park Lane. Sweeping past the palace, he unhesitatingly turned into Buckingham Gate, and thence into Victoria Street.

While they paused at the corner, Bryce saw him eyeing The Albert public house, and thought he discerned a sigh of regret. The DCS smiled, and spoke for the first time since leaving St John's Wood.

"One of your watering holes, Drummond?"

"No, sir; I've never been inside. It always

looks a nice sort of tavern, though."

"It does. A miracle it's still standing, after all the devastation hereabouts in the blitz. Perhaps we'll find the time to have a drink in there before long. Unique atmosphere in my opinion; and the bars are effectively as they were at the end of the last century. I believe The Albert was built on the site of an even older pub called The Blue Coat Boy.

"Anyway, I approve of your driving, Drummond. Just one question," he added as the car turned off the Embankment. "Do you smoke?"

"No sir," replied the constable, pleased with the unexpected praise for his driving prowess, but surprised at the even more unexpected question.

"Good, there's hope for you," Bryce said cryptically.

In the building, he instructed Drummond to see if Haig and Kittow had returned, and if so to bring them upstairs with him.

Both officers had in fact returned not ten minutes before, and were having a chat. Drummond passed on his instruction, and the three men took the stairs to Bryce's office. On the way up, Drummond told Kittow about the Chief Superintendent's question. Haig and Kittow laughed.

"The Chief is dead set against smoking, laddie," said Haig. He won't have anyone light up in his car. Did you pass that test?"

"Flying colours, I hope sir – I don't smoke at all and never have. But then he's set me another test; I have to visit and report on eight different stations on the top end of the Piccadilly Line."

His colleagues laughed again. Just as they approached Bryce's door, Haig whispered:

"He's very keen on railways – so am I, actually. And he has a serious interest in architecture too. So, as he hinted to you when giving you the Arnos Grove task, there are things to observe; do your best to spot them!"

He tapped on the door, and the three went in.

"Take seats, gentlemen. Right, Drummond, I've heard from you already, but just tell the others what you found at Arnos Grove."

The DC gave his simple report quickly and well.

"Kittow, what about you?"

Again, the report was delivered efficiently, Kittow making no attempt to disguise his opinion of Sergeant Bailey. He handed over Barratt's letter and its protective envelope, together with the address book he had removed from the dead man's house. He concluded by explaining what he had learned from Barratt's solicitor.

"Good; we'll come back to that later. What about you, Inspector?"

"Pleased to say I had a better experience in Putney than Kittow had in Tonbridge. I found the local Inspector both pleasant and competent."

Haig summarised his interview with Galbraith. "Here's his letter," he said, handing the missive in its covering envelope to Bryce. "Same as the others in style.

"Galbraith gave me the names of his previous servants, and I've got an address book from his flat. Nothing else of interest at Galbraith's – nor among Crossland's belongings, other than these two examples of his semi-literate writing."

Bryce gave his own report. "I saw the Bishop this morning. Polite sort of chap, but Lord Hartley's comment about not choosing to take a drink with the fellow immediately came to mind and struck a chord with me.

"Anyway, he insists he never accepted a bribe, and that he was perfectly entitled to sell off some redundant church plate. He described it as insignificant, and said the money went where it was needed – to boost the church restoration fund.

"We could probably check all of that, but I'm not sure that anything hinges on it. What is of interest is who knew about the sale; I've asked him to provide a list of names.

"Later, Drummond and I saw the sixth recipient, Dr Marlowe. He's adamant that there's no plagiarism in either his doctoral thesis or in his published work. He floated the theory that perhaps his letter was sent to the wrong target. I must say that is a possibility. What did you think, Drummond?"

"I agree with you, sir. I'd say he was genuine in his denials. And he didn't seem too worried about anything else that might come out in another letter."

"Yes, that's an important point for us: who we think is worried about further revelations, and who isn't.

"We can't interrogate Barratt, but we can deduce that he was sufficiently worried by the contents of the first letter.

"Ditto Galbraith. For both those men it's possible that the first allegation was so bad that anything else wouldn't have made things worse for them.

"As for the first three – the Westminster men – they all claim not to be worried by their letter, but none had really taken in the possibility of further allegations. When that was suggested, I'm not sure that there wasn't a frisson of concern from each of them, despite emphatic statements that they wouldn't pay even if more allegations followed."

Bryce offered the floor to his team. "Can we draw any conclusions from any of that?"

Kittow spoke first. "I don't really think so, sir. It seems to me that it doesn't much matter whether or not any fresh allegations are more serious for the victim. I think new allegations will only be relevant to us because they may throw up more clues, which might give us another chance to find out how the blackmailer got his information."

"Aye, that last point is important," acknowledged Haig. "But I think you're missing something about the worries of the victims, Kittow. If the next accusations are more damaging to the recipients, surely there must be a danger that they won't tell us about new letters – much less show them to us? We won't know about fresh clues if we don't get to see the letters."

"Yes, I see all of that for the first three recipients, sir," said Drummond turning to Haig, and surprised to hear himself speaking so easily to his Inspector. "But even if that happens, the local boys will keep a look-out, so we'd still get to see new letters addressed to Galbraith and Barratt, wouldn't we? And I'm sure Dr Marlowe will hand his over, if he gets one. There may be extra clues about the blackmailer's identity that we could pick up in new correspondence to those three men – even if the three big names won't hand over theirs."

"All good thoughts, gentlemen," said Bryce. "The Inspector makes a valid point about frightening the Westminster trio. But Drummond, I'd be surprised if the links between our top three and the blackmailer aren't more crucial than anything relating to the other three. Of the six men we know of so far, they're certainly the ones with the furthest to fall.

"Tasks for tomorrow. All steady background work to begin with, and we'll see what leads that throws up."

Pocketbooks and pencils appeared. Bryce allocated Haig the two address books and shared the lists of the names so far collected between the two detectives constables. An initial cross-checking of names was to be carried out in an attempt to establish a firm link between any of the blackmailed parties, after which secretaries, servants, and brokers were all to be scrutinised as discreetly as possible, including checking for criminal records.

"Take Crossland, for example. We'll assume he didn't write the letters, but there must be a chance Galbraith was right, and that it was the valet who passed on the information. We need to know how he was recruited to his post. If it was an agency, which is quite probable, who else do they have on their books who might work for one of the other victims – or who might have worked for them in the past?

"Somewhere there's a connection between these six people and the blackmailer – see how quickly you can find it.

"In the meantime, I'll get hold of Marlowe's professor and see whether he agrees with his

scholar's opinion about not being a plagiarist.
 "Meet here again at ten o'clock tomorrow."

CHAPTER 12

Friday 3rd November, 1950

In the morning, just before nine o'clock, the agreed plan changed. A messenger from Scotland Yard's post room arrived in the new Chief Superintendent's office bearing a familiar-looking azure envelope addressed to:

The Officer In Charge of Blackmail Cases

"Come in the first post, sir. Word is you're workin' on this," said the chirpy youngster.

"Yes, it's my problem, Reeves; thank you," said Bryce, pointing to where the envelope should be placed on his desk so that he didn't have to touch it.

Picking up the internal telephone, he called Haig. "Come up immediately, please, Inspector. We have a letter, which could be from Nemesis. Bring the fingerprint gear, and you may as well get Kittow and Drummond up here at the same time."

The DCS replaced the receiver and eyed the envelope malevolently. If this was indeed from the author of the six earlier letters, he felt it was likely to complicate matters.

As he waited for his colleagues, Bryce asked himself what sort of blackmailer would communicate directly with the police. He knew murderers and hoaxers sometimes did so, in order to mock the Force – the Jack the Ripper *'Dear Boss'* letter, and the *'Saucy Jacky'* postcard, being perhaps the most infamous examples of such communications. But he had no knowledge or experience of blackmailers, or blackmail hoaxers, who engaged with the police.

His three subordinates trooped in together.

Bryce waved at the envelope. "Addressed to Scotland Yard and posted to catch the evening collection from a box at Euston this time, not Arnos Grove. Let Kittow check for prints, Inspector, under your supervision.

"Kittow, if you satisfy the Inspector's gimlet eye and meet his high standards today, you can consider yourself qualified to do this work unsupervised in future, and start training Drummond."

"Quite a lot of different prints, sir," announced Kittow a few minutes later when he had dusted both sides of the envelope. "Mostly smudged, or on top of others."

"Inevitable. One set will be from young Reeves in the post room for a start. Get him to provide exclusion prints later, and retain what's left. Not much hope, of course, because we already know our blackmailer is careful, as well as clever," said Bryce as he pushed a pair of tweezers across to Kittow.

Once neatly extracted, the detectives immediately noticed the communication was several pages long, whereas the blackmail letters so far seen were only a single sheet. Haig nodded to Kittow to get busy again.

No one was surprised when the powder revealed no prints at all.

"You've already got mucky fingers, Kittow; read the letter aloud for us, please," instructed Bryce.

The DC cleared his throat.

Dear Sir

You will no doubt be surprised to hear from me, but circumstances have changed and I am forced to adapt.

I wrote to ten men. Each was instructed not to contact the police. I now learn that at least three of them did so. In the next few days I shall ascertain if any of the other seven failed to heed my clear instructions.

Not that it really matters.

I should explain to you that financial gain was never my purpose. My intention from the outset was to publicise certain facts and thus humiliate, and ultimately ruin, these hypocrites who hold themselves up as decent and worthwhile members of society. The inclusion of a pecuniary demand was simply a device by which to maintain the impression of blackmail, and that my silence could be bought. It cannot.

Indeed, although I initially mentioned money, the risk to me in arranging for payment would always be far too great. No, I simply wanted to draw out the process of instilling fear in these men, before eventually exposing them to the world for what they really are.

I shall deal first with those men who, I believe, have disobeyed my instructions – the three who all take some part in the governance of our country. I have written again to each, giving more details. As it is quite possible that none of them will wish to contact the police a second time, being rightly fearful of arrest, I am also informing you of the facts.

Before I turn to those facts, you should know that I have not told the three that I am simultaneously contacting the police. Naturally, I regret that I won't be able to witness the inevitable games of cat and mouse when you ask to see the new letters and the craven three pretend they haven't received one! Still, even though I shan't see that jolly sport, I do hope it will afford you some amusement. (After all, what is life if one cannot enjoy a laugh?)

First, David Poole. It is, I suppose, almost a truism that a politician must have mendacious tendencies. However, cynic though I am, I don't believe that the majority of our parliamentarians are criminals. Poole certainly is.

I know that in 1937 he bought (I use the word advisedly) at least five members of the committee of his local constituency party. He thus ensured his adoption as candidate. As the constituency is one which seems unlikely ever to change its political colour, it also guaranteed his election to Parliament.

I have pointed out how he accepted money for influencing support towards those companies prepared to grease his grasping palms. Those dealings provided the funds which enabled him to become very wealthy so quickly. That wealth, in turn, endowed him with the veneer of corporate competence which propelled his political success.

Most unedifying behaviour for a public servant – especially as he was a Government minister at the time.

I am not a lawyer, and it may be that no criminal offence was committed. But I hardly think his local party, or the Prime Minister, will be able to ignore it when the information is made public.

Far more serious, however, is this. In November 1945 he accepted a significant bribe of seven hundred pounds from a constituent. Following which, Poole in turn bribed a local police Inspector to drop the investigation into an allegation of rape levelled against the son of the constituent who bribed him. That police officer has recently retired. He was paid three hundred pounds. I think he may now choose to co-operate. I shall provide his name in a later communication.

Second, Peregrine Hartley. I find it beyond distasteful that a man who profiteered throughout the Great War should be rewarded, first with a knighthood and not long after with a peerage. We all know how such honours were almost openly traded at the time, of course. But the fact that his wartime profiteering formed the foundation of his fortune, and therefore his ability to subsequently purchase his honours, sickens me.

And, just as a leopard never changes its spots, Hartley made equally obscene profits out of the last war.

In my first letter, just to get his attention, I accused him of using privileged information to buy and sell stocks. Not, I admit, an illegal activity as the law stands. I expect he has brushed the matter off accordingly. But to those of us whose nostrils haven't been completely corrupted by the reek of too much money, it leaves a distinct smell.

I will also reveal that between 1906 and 1912 he was involved – as the prime mover – in at least three sophisticated cases of long firm fraud. Several people lost money; two were ruined. Hartley profited enormously. There were token police investigations, none of which got anywhere. My experience leads me to believe that he had a penchant for bribery – he certainly bought his honours. Regrettably I cannot prove that he ever bought the police, as Poole did.

Nevertheless, in the next few days I shall provide you with the names of the fraudulent companies, together with sufficient information to connect Hartley to them, incontrovertibly.

Finally, Caspar Charrington. Not elected to any office but, like Hartley, with a seat in the Upper House. There, he can, and does, pontificate on secular matters. Hypocrisy is always nauseating, but when found in a man of the cloth...need I say more?

Whatever lies he told you, he did accept money for conferring a church position. I shall provide further details of that, with the name of the beneficiary, in a later communication.

Again, he did sell items belonging to his parish, and I do not believe he had the authority to do so.

It is possible that both those transgressions might only be pursuable in the ecclesiastical courts. The next, however, is criminal, and will ensure his long-overdue downfall.

Some twenty years ago, when he was vicar of that same Dorset parish, he carried out the most serious of assaults on at least two choirboys.

In my next communication, I shall give you the names of those involved – now men in their thirties. At least one, and I believe both, will co-operate. The parents are still living, and can tell you what their sons cannot: how the matter was hushed up at the time before Charrington moved on to higher office.

There you have it.

I shall consider the other seven men in due

course. I admit that they haven't annoyed me to the same extent as these three, given that none of them has a place in running the country and none of them purports to be fit for such a role.

In the case of one, I even have a degree of sympathy, as he and I are 'kindred spirits'. (Indeed, in his particular case I should never have written him a letter at all, were it not for his turning police informant and ruining two other men's lives).

It may be that those who obeyed my instructions not to contact the police will be let off with a warning – I haven't yet decided.

Yours faithfully,
A latter-day Nemesis

Kittow looked up and saw his three colleagues staring at the letter, as if they were re-reading the lines he had just spoken.

"Thank you," said Bryce. "Apart from the fresh allegations, which we'll come back to later, what, if anything, can we glean from this latest epistle?"

"He enjoys twisting the knife, that's for sure!" said Drummond.

"Aye," agreed Haig. "And how does he know that some of these people contacted the police, sir?"

"A very good question, Inspector. And he writes about considering what to do with the other seven; so it seems he doesn't know about Marlowe contacting us, and hasn't yet learned about Barratt and Galbraith. That again, incidentally, goes some way to support Galbraith's idea that his valet was the source of his master's private information."

"But Hartley's matter arose before the Great War, sir," objected Kittow. "Surely it's not likely that a servant would still be around to report that now?"

"Very true; I can't quibble with that. Something to think about, certainly."

"He tells us what we guessed but didn't know for sure – that even more people had letters," said Drummond.

"Yes. Although as they may now be 'forgiven', I don't propose to spend time trying to find them, unless we make no headway with the six we're already looking into," said Bryce.

"What about this business of not really wanting money at all," asked Haig. "Could that be just a belated ploy to avoid a blackmail conviction if he's caught?"

Bryce was doubtful. "If it is, I'm not sure it would be successful. The threat demanding money has already been uttered in all of the cases we're looking at.

"In a prosecution, the Crown might also argue that money isn't an essential element of blackmail. The Larceny Act says that any valuable property or thing will suffice. Someone's 'good name' might be considered a valuable thing, although no doubt the defence would try and counter that by arguing that the victim's loss of reputation didn't become a 'gain', as such, for the blackmailer.

"All of us have used the pronoun 'he' for our blackmailer. From the outset, and without cause, really, we've all assumed that the author is a man. David Poole picked up on the point, and I've thought about it since. In both Greek and Roman mythology, Nemesis is a goddess. Would a man adopt the persona of a female?"

"To be honest, sir, I didn't know Nemesis was female," said Kittow. "Isn't it used as a general comeuppance name, without anyone really needing to know about the goddess part? Alternatively, could it be a sort of double bluff – make us think it's a woman, when it's really a man?"

"Bryce nodded. "You're right. But it's made me open my eyes to at least the possibility that we have a vengeful woman – as Poole suggested earlier.

"Anyway, I think I'll get someone else to take a look at this letter. There's no handwriting to analyse, but I know a psychologist who might give an opinion based on the choice of words and so on. The writer has a very precise style, but whether that trait is more common among men than women I have no idea.

"Let's consider the new revelations. What about Hartley?"

"Sorry, sir," said Drummond, diffidently

raising his hand as though in school. "I've no idea what 'long firm fraud' is."

"It's a slang term really, there's no such offence in law, although the action is a larceny. The practice has been known to go on since the eighteenth century.

"I'll give you an example. A new limited company is set up. It buys small quantities of goods from a manufacturer or wholesaler – all on credit. Invoices are presented and paid very promptly. Do that a few times and the new company rapidly appears creditworthy to the supplier.

"However, after a while, a much larger order is submitted. The goods are delivered as usual, but this time no payment is made. Weeks probably pass before enquiries reveal that the new company has disappeared, along with the goods. Those are sold off elsewhere and the crook takes all of the profit without any of the purchase costs."

"I can see how easy it would be to make money really quickly like that. But can Lord Hartley still be prosecuted for something that happened over forty years ago?" asked Kittow.

"In theory, yes. We don't have a general statute of limitations like some other countries. In practice, though, many witnesses will be dead or otherwise incapacitated and unable to testify. Even if they're living and capable, their recollections would be easily questioned in court. I also doubt if bank records could be produced. A lot will depend on the strength of evidence our author provides, but I wouldn't bet on this ever coming to trial."

The DCS invited his team to consider the Government minister next. "What about Poole? Any feelings about him?"

"If it's true he bribed a police officer to turn a blind eye, it's unforgivable, and he should go down," said Haig, "and I'd like to think something would happen to the police officer, too, even if he is retired now." Kittow and Drummond nodded in agreement.

"Yes," said Bryce, "and the whole business is made more heinous because of the offence that was allegedly covered up. I think the bribery between Poole and the police officer will only rank as misdemeanours under the Public Bodies Corrupt Practices Act. If the allegation is true, hopefully some bright prosecuting lawyer can think of a more substantial charge.

"But irrespective of whether there's enough evidence to charge him, if this gets into the public domain – and we're told today that is the author's only intention – I think this marks the end of Poole's political career.

"Assuming the latest allegation is based on fact, what about the Bishop's case?"

The facial expressions spoke for their owners. "Castration's too good," muttered Haig, with Kittow and Drummond again agreeing.

"I think," said Bryce, "that if the author comes up with the necessary details, this would be the easiest of the three matters to prove.

"However, gentlemen, I must remind you that at the moment we're not actually here to investigate any of these alleged offences – we're investigating blackmail. I intend to take advice from the AC on this, but we may have to pass everything else to other officers."

"You mean the more we learn about the actions of the blackmailer's victims, the less seriously we might start to view the blackmail itself, sir?" asked Haig.

"Exactly, Inspector. When this eventually hits the press, I don't doubt that the overwhelming majority of the readers will take that view as well.

"But we can't adopt that line ourselves. Barratt has committed suicide because of the blackmail letter he received, and Galbraith killed someone who may be quite innocent of any involvement at all. And even if he wasn't innocent, Crossland didn't deserve a summary death penalty.

"At this stage, we've seen no evidence to back up these more serious allegations, and the three individuals must be presumed innocent unless or until proved otherwise.

"I often say 'I'm not a betting man', but then go on to offer a wager on something. I wonder what odds I should offer here on whether one, two, three – or none – of the Westminster trio report their new letters?"

Broad smiles were the responses to Bryce's imaginary 'book'.

"I'd have an each-way bet and put money on none, or the one that looks least likely to have a criminal case against him," said Kittow.

"Agreed," said Haig, "and my 'one' would be Hartley, for the same reason."

"I can't afford to bet," said Drummond, "but I agree with the Inspector."

Bryce laughed. "Well, if I was a bookmaker I wouldn't do very well out of this. You're all betting on the same runner, and it's the one I'd put my own money on!

"All right; carry on with trying to find out about these secretaries, servants, agencies, and so on. I'm not going to contact our recipients again just yet; give them time to receive their letters and have a think."

CHAPTER 13

Had the officers been able to find a bookmaker, they would all have had a win to celebrate, because an hour later, Bryce picked up his telephone and heard Hartley's voice. The noble lord was not a happy man, uttering several coarse epithets while ranting that the Commissioner wouldn't take his call.

"Nothing against you, Chief Superintendent, but in my position I expect to deal with the top man, not his bloody minions."

"I did tell you that he wouldn't talk to you again, m'lord," said Bryce, momentarily ignoring the insulting reference to himself. "It's not personal – he won't speak to the other parties concerned. And I shan't speak to you either, if you don't moderate your language!"

Bryce heard what sounded like a strangled enraged yelp at the other end of the line, followed by a few deep breaths. A calmer-sounding Hartley eventually spoke.

"I've received another letter from the blackguard. I'll tell you what it says…"

"No need," interrupted Bryce. "I can save you the bother because I probably know what it says. The author was bold enough to write to Scotland Yard about it."

"What? Oh, God! Well, you'll know that he's out to completely ruin my reputation. Says he's never actually been interested in money. What do I do?"

"If you could get the letter and its envelope to me via special messenger, I'd be obliged."

"Very well; I'll arrange that," growled the peer. "And what are you going to do about these ridiculous fraud allegations, eh?" Hartley's tone was challenging. If the Commissioner refused his approaches, he intended to hold up as many hoops as he wished, and ensure the Chief Superintendent jumped through every one of them.

"Nothing," was Bryce's level reply. "I assume the writer told you he will provide more detailed information soon. If that includes any actual evidence, I shall review my decision. In the meantime, have you thought any more about how the blackmailer obtained all this information about you?"

Hartley was infuriated by this refusal to jump through even the first of his hoops, but realised he was unable to do anything about it. He let loose his anger again.

"That's a damn fool question, man – I've thought of little else! It's all lies and naked character assassination. It's unbelievable to me that you're not doing anything constructive to help me, instead of wasting your time on something that didn't happen forty years ago!"

The expression 'frothing at the mouth' sprang to Bryce's ears, and he imagined that flecks of spittle were landing on the peer's telephone handset.

The DCS remained at his most polite in the face of this tirade. "Forty years is certainly a long time ago, m'lord, but what I tell you next might help your memory. We've learned that a man named Julian Barratt has committed suicide. His letter from Nemesis accused him of fraud. You were named as his accomplice. Did you know him?"

Lord Hartley said nothing, but a slow exhalation of breath at the other end of the line told Bryce the peer hadn't hung up. He repeated the question.

"The name doesn't ring a bell," said Hartley at last.

"I see. Well, please continue to think of how all this information leaked to the letter-writer. We're obviously trying to check any connections between staff and other contacts. Perhaps there may be more helpful information when the author approaches you – or us – again."

"Not likely to be helpful to me, blast you!" snarled the peer rudely. "What do you think he's going to do next?"

"I really don't know. If he's serious about not wanting any money, then all he wants to cause you – and the others – is as much anguish as possible before informing the newspapers."

"Not just me, then?"

"No; not just you."

"Hummph. That old stuff he's trying to dredge up – it's all vindictive fabrication and fantasy, Chief Superintendent."

"As I'm only charged with looking into the blackmail aspect, it's not my concern anyway, m'lord."

Bryce added a quiet "At least, not yet it isn't" to himself, after he said 'goodbye' to Hartley and replaced his receiver.

***

Having spent some time on paperwork associated with other cases, the DCS decided to break up his pen-pushing tasks and make the telephone call to Marlowe's mentor. Marlowe had mentioned his Cambridge college, and Bryce belatedly remembered hearing about the man during his own time in the city. He set his Secretary to make some calls around the university, to ascertain where the Professor might be found.

It took her almost half an hour to discover that McGrath was now professor emeritus. Conveniently, though, he could now be found in London, working with the Natural History

Museum after retiring from his university chair. A call to that institution produced a promise that Professor McGrath would ring back when he could be located.

Happy to wait, Bryce employed himself in emptying his 'in' tray. That job well done, he settled down with a fresh pad of paper, thinking it was time to consider how he would like his new fiefdom to operate.

The latitude that he had been given – that he would be able to build his new branch of the organisation almost unfettered – was unprecedented for someone of his rank. Even more extraordinary was the implication that he was free to select men for promotions.

After four years at the Yard, Bryce was only too aware of some of the deficiencies within the CID. Before settling on Haig as his 'bagman', he had tried out and rejected two other detective sergeants. Neither was incompetent, but they didn't approach the standard he wanted.

However, among all the ranks from detective constable upwards, there were a few men that he did consider incompetent. Others he classified as idle, or possessing a bad attitude to the job. He mentally added Yapp to that latter small group. Having been given the chance, there must be a clearing of dead wood.

Bryce welcomed the fact that he was expected to continue as an operational detective as much as possible. As the AC had pointed out, he would need a good administrator for his departmental second-in-command. That individual would need to have the respect of the others in the department as far as his detective skills were concerned. However, there were two other attributes which for this post might be even more important. The first was to be good at paperwork. But above all the man must not be someone who avoided making the right decision because it might be unpopular.

He mentally reviewed the DCIs remaining after his own promotion. When the soon-to-retire officer dealing with Yapp was removed from the running, he was left with only two prospects. The first was a walking disaster, and Bryce resolved to get rid of him somehow. The second was a comparatively young and very competent detective. It would be a bad move to take him away from field work.

Bryce started to run through the current detective inspectors. Again, a mixed bag. One name immediately came to mind, but he put it aside and reviewed all the others of that rank he could think of – including those in other branches.

His thoughts were interrupted by the telephone. Picking up the handset, a cultured voice spoke.

"McGrath here – somebody wants me?"

Bryce introduced himself. "Sorry to disturb you, Professor, it's a sensitive matter

I need to speak to you about. There's been an attempt to blackmail one of your old students – Simon Marlowe – citing plagiarism in his doctoral thesis, and also in a subsequent published work. Dr Marlowe has given me your name to support him on the first matter. Can you help at all?"

A loud belly-laugh came down the telephone line.

"Someone's pulling your leg, Chief Superintendent! I can say without fear of contradiction that Marlowe's thesis was original work throughout. There is absolutely no question of plagiarism.

"I didn't work with him on his book, but of course I know it well. His central premise was so novel that I doubt if anyone else in our field had ever even thought about it. No, I can safely tell you that if anybody, anywhere in the world, has published anything like it, I haven't seen it.

"Naturally, some old feathers in the establishment were rubbed up the wrong way. Always happens when the young bloods start advancing their own ideas," continued McGrath, "but blackmail? Extraordinary!"

"Well, thank you Professor; very helpful."

"Not at all, I'm glad to be of some use. Am I right in thinking that I saw you speak at the Union once – 1933 or thereabouts?"

"You're quite right, Professor, although as we lost the debate I've tried to forget about it!"

McGrath laughed again. "As I recall, you were every inch a barrister in the making. An old friend – a law professor – sitting with me that night predicted great things for you at the bar. What changed your mind – not just miffed at losing that debate, surely?"

It was Bryce's turn to laugh. "I can guess who the man with the faulty crystal ball was; please give him my regards when you next see him.

"No, I was called to the bar, but I found the reality of life as junior counsel wasn't what I'd expected, and I was impatient, I suppose. The Trenchard entry scheme became available, so I joined the Met instead."

"Well, best of luck with your case, Bryce. Marlowe isn't everyone's cup of tea; I remember he irritated a few people at Cambridge after a couple of the boat races. That old trope: 'if there's one thing worse than a bad loser it's a bad winner', comes to mind. He had a tendency to crow rather too loudly and rather too long when his team triumphed. Always managed to make it sound as though his stroke alone was the deciding factor. His book made him rather more unpopular amongst the fraternity, I don't doubt. But plagiarist he is not."

Bryce had hardly returned to his planning, when a knock on his door produced Inspector Haig.

"Welcome," said Bryce, "and sit down. I've

a couple of things to tell you, and presumably you have something for me?"

"Aye, we've been cross-checking with one another downstairs and we've found a possible connection, sir. There's a domestic and general staff bureau called Coates in Lower Regent Street. Not an old outfit; it was only set up a month or so after the war. But it seems to have developed a decent reputation in the last few years.

"They claim to be able to supply everyone from butlers to gardeners and whoever else might be wanted in between those two. Given that good staff are hard to find these days, they seem to have gained a fair chunk of the market by producing exactly what an employer wants. Not just around London, but all over. And they've bought out at least two other domestic agencies.

"Crossland was recruited through Coates. So was a footman currently employed by Poole at his London residence – and that man transfers to Poole's country house when the minister goes there for any length of time.

"There's also a Coates man employed at the Bishop's palace. And that's a long way from London."

Bryce was pleased. "Good work, Inspector. However, if as you say this agency has almost cornered the market, we probably shouldn't be too surprised that our recipients used the same agency."

"True enough, sir. But there's one other

link which might be important," said Haig. "This only came up by pure accident, but Lord Hartley's personal secretary, Burnett, also employs a valet, a man called Hobbs. Placed by one of the established agencies that Coates swallowed up."

Bryce mulled this over. "Interesting. If the valet is involved it might provide a link via Burnett's father to a time before the Great War. Tenuous, but as you say, a link nevertheless.

"Let me just tell you what I've learned, Inspector," said the DCS. He briefly ran through his call with Hartley, and Professor McGrath's report on Marlowe.

"Hartley said Julian Barratt's name didn't ring a bell. I couldn't see his face, of course, but he was slow to answer and I believe he was lying."

A thought suddenly occurred to Bryce. "Hang on a minute." He picked up the internal telephone and dialled the CID office. "Kittow, come up right away," he ordered.

The DC arrived promptly.

"Kittow, you didn't mention servants at Barratt's place, but I'm pretty sure the AC said he had two. Did you see any while you were there?"

"No sir," said Kittow in surprise. "Sergeant Bailey had the front door key and he let us in. The house was empty, and no one came while we were there."

"Right. We need to track these two down.

Get on to an officer of your rank at Tonbridge, Inspector. Completely bypass the sergeant who didn't help Kittow – I'm minded to make a complaint about him, but that's a job for another day. See what you can find out about the two missing staff.

"Kittow, you've got Barratt's address book. Try and make contact with his former wife. I know Bailey told you the Lancashire boys were going to tell her about her ex-husband's demise, but be a bit careful what you say until you're sure she's heard. I want to know as many details as possible of all staff they might have employed during their marriage, and how they found them.

Bryce grinned at Haig. "If one or both of the two came via Coates, I'll begin to be convinced that you've turned up a good lead, Inspector.

"Take Kittow downstairs with you now and find Drummond; brief him about Hartley and Marlowe, and carry on digging, all of you," was Bryce's parting instruction.

***

A few minutes after four o'clock, Haig rang his boss to request a short team discussion. Glad of the diversion from his 'in' tray, which had filled again in the short time since he had emptied it, Bryce readily agreed.

The four men were soon sitting with the

tea Bryce's secretary had brought.

"I'll start off by telling you that neither the Bishop nor Poole has been in contact, and I'm not at all pleased about it," said the DCS. "I'll stir them both up tomorrow – I could just do with upsetting someone!"

When the laughter had died down Haig said, "We have a bit of news, sir. The Tonbridge DI was far more helpful than his Sergeant, and he's been busy on our behalf. He called at a couple of Barratt's neighbours and spoke to the domestics there. It seems the man did have two live-in servants: a cook-housekeeper and a general maid.

"One of the neighbouring servants had been friendly with Mrs Marwick, Barratt's cook. She had her friend's new address – gone to live with a sister in Ashford.

"Apparently, Barratt dismissed both of them only hours before killing himself. Told them the house would be sold because he was going on a long journey – a statement true in its way. He was very generous with the payoff; gave each of them a hundred pounds on top of three months wages in lieu. He told the women they had to leave the same day.

"The friend said that Mrs Marwick was ready to retire, and the extra money helped decide her. She'd been with Barratt for years, originally engaged by Mrs Barratt through an advertisement in *The Lady*. But the maid, Aggie

Saunders, only arrived about a year ago, soon after the wife left. She was engaged through the Coates agency."

"Where are these women now?" asked Bryce.

"The DI got officers in Ashford to call on Mrs Marwick, and she told them Aggie's living with her mother in Whitechapel again, until she can find another post. Got her address, too."

"Good. So Aggie doesn't know we're interested yet?"

"Probably not, sir. She may not even know Barratt is dead."

"Even better. How about you, Kittow? Any other progress?"

"I spoke to Mrs Barratt, sir. The Lancashire boys had called and told her about her husband, so that was all right. She'd originally taken on Mrs Marwick, but she didn't have details for any others so it probably won't be easy to track them.

"She did say something that struck me, though. Her husband had started to behave oddly over the years and although he wouldn't tell her what was wrong, he occasionally talked about 'his dreadful guilt' and about 'making his peace with God'. She said he gradually became more and more wrapped up in himself and strange, and eventually she couldn't stand it and left him."

"Guilt, eh? And over a period of time. Interesting," mused Bryce. "I assumed the letter linking him with Hartley referred to some fairly recent fraud. But I suppose Barratt would be the right age to have worked with Hartley before the Great War – so he could have been involved in the long firm frauds. He might be an even more plausible link to that era than Douglas Burnett's father."

Bryce sat back and studied his ceiling for a minute whilst his men waited expectantly.

"I'm a bit worried about jumping to conclusions regarding this employment agency. All our eggs seem to be in one basket, and – to mix metaphors horribly – there's no proof that one of them is bad.

"Also, just suppose it's the domestics who've been gathering the information, and that the level of their literacy is similar to Galbraith's valet, Crossland. To whom do they supply the information? Who's the person paying them for it? And crucially, is the person who pays for it our blackmailer – because if it isn't, how does it get to him?"

"We'll definitely have to talk to all the staff who came to the victims' houses via Coates, but we need to nab as many of them as possible at the same time – surprise them all.

"I'm not quite ready to spring that on them just yet; I want to find out a bit more about the bureau first. And I want that done discreetly and unofficially – nothing whatsoever to do with the police on the face of it."

The Chief Superintendent regarded his subordinates, then beamed at DC Drummond. "Have you ever trodden the boards, Constable? School plays or amateur dramatics, perhaps?"

Completely taken aback at this sudden shift in focus, it took Drummond a moment to understand what was being proposed.

"Do you want me to apply for a job through Coates, sir?"

"I do! You'll have to admit that you have no experience, of course, so don't go saying you want to be a butler. Just be eager and enthusiastic; tell them you're prepared to start at the bottom."

"What about checks on Drummond, sir?" asked Kittow, much relieved that he hadn't been selected for the task, as memories of his five-year-old self dropping the 'myrrh' in his infants' Nativity play (and later receiving a slap on the back of his legs with a wooden ruler) came back to him. "If they've got such a thick slice of the domestic staff market now, they can't be a complete shower of an outfit; they're bound to do some sort of check."

Bryce nodded, "Yes, you're right, Kittow." He looked at Drummond again. "Do you have a friend, one who's in a lowly sort of job already, and perhaps looking to change? Your own age, ideally?"

"I do, sir, as it happens; a couple in fact. One of them's been wondering if he might apply to join the Met. I reckon he'd definitely help out if I ask him."

"Better and better! You can tell him from me that if he's suitable in all other ways I shall put in a good word for him when the time comes. Find him tonight, and see if you can borrow his name and address. Explain very briefly what it's about, but don't mention Coates. He doesn't have to do anything himself, except pass on any communication which might come to his address.

"If he agrees, go along to the agency first thing on Monday morning, armed with his identity card and his previous employment record. Under the pretence of wanting a job, check how things work at Coates. If they ask about references, keep it vague. Say you'll speak to an old teacher, or a doctor, or something. Understand?"

Drummond nodded. "I'm sure my mate will co-operate," he said, before checking an important point with his boss. "He won't be prosecuted for lending me his ID card, will he?"

"No, no," laughed Haig. "We might prosecute you for carrying false ID, though!"

Drummond grinned and started to make mental plans as to how he would play his part in the Coates office.

After his men had gone back to their desks, Bryce called the AC's office on the off chance that his boss was still in. Finding that he was, the DCS asked for an appointment and was told to come up right away.

***

Bryce was at the AC's door within a minute of putting down the telephone. The secretary waved him straight in to the inner office.

"Hello, Philip. How are you getting on?" asked the senior man.

"I suppose we're making progress, sir, but it's slow. I assume you don't want details at this stage?"

"No, I leave it to you. But you're after something, obviously," he said, smiling.

"Advice on one point sir, and a query on another," said Bryce as he took a chair.

"First, it seems that the blackmailer may be accurate regarding the allegations made. If that is confirmed, some of the so-called victims are at risk of being prosecuted for serious offences. As they must be, frankly, if the evidence is forthcoming.

"And before you ask, sir, yes – the three Westminster men are in that category.

"While blackmail is an ugly crime, I have to say that what we've uncovered so far suggests that the blackmailer could almost be said to be working in the public interest.

"He has now written to the police, saying he's waiving his claim to money, and that as far as Hartley and company are concerned, humiliation and ruin is his aim. In my view he – or she – is still guilty of attempted blackmail, though.

"What I'd like advice on is this. As we go along with the investigation, if evidence emerges as I think it will, should I pass what we might call the secondary offences to other officers? Or should I treat those as part of the original blackmail case?

"Never heard of a blackmailer contacting the police – this is certainly a strange case." The AC pondered the matter further. "Seems a bit pointless to ask other officers to investigate these new matters, when your team is finding the initial evidence," he said at last. "If you find more evidence – enough to arrest someone on suspicion, or even just enough to invite someone to come and 'help with enquiries' – then I suggest you should follow the case through. Doesn't stop you charging the blackmailer."

"Thank you, sir, that's cleared that up, although I suppose it's possible that I might get the other evidence while still unable to identify the blackmailer.

"My second matter is to do with the reorganisation, sir. Early days, of course. The other day you indicated that I'd be given quite a bit of autonomy. I really need to know, if possible, how far that extends. For example, you said that I would be able to submit names for promotion, and there are two or three worthy cases that I'll be suggesting to you soon."

The AC smiled. I can't give you *carte blanche* on promotions, Philip. But I know you well enough to realise that you won't be putting up your useless old friends – even if you had any! Let's put it this way. Budget permitting, I'm very unlikely to turn down any of your proposals. All I'm saying is, best not promise anything without clearing it with me first."

"I really appreciate that, sir. The next matter might be a bit more delicate. You also hinted about my being able to clear out dead wood. I have two or three names in that category. Is it realistic to think that my suggestions will be acted on?"

The AC smiled. "Giving colleagues the chop is a big responsibility, and I understand your desire to check the reach and sharpness of your axe! Off the record, the Commissioner himself believes there should be a purge. Frankly, that's one of the reasons you've been given this job. Let me put it this way. If you come to me with names and reasons, it's highly probable that you'll be backed to the hilt."

Bryce left the AC's office very well satisfied. He returned to his own room, and called Haig on the internal telephone.

"I'll be coming in for a while in the morning, Inspector, but you and the others don't need to do the same. I'll see you all on Monday morning – wish Drummond well for his performance at Coates!"

"Matter of fact, sir, Drummond is coming in himself tomorrow morning. Says he has a couple of statements to do on other cases and he hasn't had time to do them in the last few days.

"Fair enough. Tell him if he's still here at twelve o'clock I'll take him to the Albert for a bite to eat."

CHAPTER 14

Saturday 4th November, 1950

Bryce arrived at his desk, half expecting to find a note saying that one of the victims had called, but there was nothing. His Secretary wasn't working, so he started making calls himself. Calculating that if the Bishop was still in London a local telephone call would be cheaper, he gave the switchboard operator the number for the Goring hotel. Here he was unlucky, the hotel receptionist informing him that "His lordship isn't in residence today". Returning to the switchboard, he gave the number for the Bishop's palace instead.

On connection he spoke to one obsequious man before being passed to a second, this one so unctuous that Bryce thought instinctively of Uriah Heep, and visualised him rubbing his hands together – before realising that such an activity would be rather difficult while holding a telephone handset.

It seemed that his lordship was meeting a delegation of some sort, and unavailable at present. However, the message to call Mr Wilson urgently would be passed on as soon as possible.

With no idea how long it would be before the call was returned – if it ever was – Bryce initiated his second call, thinking that Poole should be rather easier to track down on his home number than when in his ministry office or his Commons office.

Had Poole been at home, he would have been correct. However, Poole's wife informed him that her husband was in fact working in the ministry. Bryce rang the relevant number. The skeleton staff on duty at the weekend found it hard to locate their target. Eventually someone reported that the Minister had left the office to get some fresh air, and undertook to ask him to call Mr Wilson urgently when he returned. The DCS gave an ex-directory number rather than the public number for the Yard, and reverted to his staff planning, mildly annoyed at his inability to make immediate contact with either of his targets.

***

It was an hour-and-a half before the external telephone rang, but the caller was another overworked professional spending Saturday morning at his desk. The prosecuting solicitor in an unrelated case admitted that he was chancing his arm, and hadn't really expected to find Bryce in. The DCS dealt with that matter, and then stood up and took a few turns around the room. He had just resumed his seat when the instrument rang again.

"Chief Superintendent? David Poole here. You called me?"

"I did. Have you something to tell me?"

There was a pause. "I don't think so."

"Oh I think otherwise, Minister," said Bryce firmly. "I remind you that you called the police to complain of a blackmail attempt, on which a lot of police time has been spent already. It really doesn't do to suddenly stop co-operating; that might even amount to obstructing us in our duty."

A spluttering expostulation came from the telephone. "Do you dare to threaten me, Chief Superintendent?"

Bryce's retort was unambiguous. "Take it how you like, Minister. But be assured that if it becomes necessary I'll do more than threaten! What have you to tell me?"

"Nothing! I withdraw my complaint about the bloody letter. I shall write and complain to the Commissioner about your attitude towards a Minister of the Crown – and see that the Home Secretary gets a copy."

Bryce smiled to himself. "Do that by all means, if you wish. However, the complaint of blackmail, once registered, can't simply be withdrawn. We have evidence of blackmail against you, and the public interest suggests we should continue to look into it".

More inarticulate noises came from the handset.

"Since you decline to tell me what your letter says," continued the DCS, "I'll tell you what I believe. You received a second letter, probably yesterday, making a far more serious allegation.

"Before you deny that, Minister, perhaps I should tell you that the blackmailer has written to me, explaining a fresh allegation against you. I'm informed of two additional things, which may not have been explained to you.

"First, I shall shortly be receiving a further letter, giving the relevant names and other facts.

"Second, there is no longer any intention to extort money. Nemesis is now, apparently, simply out to ruin you.

"You can see that there is no point in trying to keep quiet about your latest letter. You are no longer able to buy silence. I'd be grateful if you would have the letter and its envelope delivered to me as soon as possible."

Poole didn't reply for a long time. Then he let out a sigh. "I see," he said at last. "Very well, I'll arrange that now.

"In the meantime, Bryce, what do you intend to do about the fresh allegation against me?"

"Nothing, at least not yet. If more detailed information emerges, giving *prima facie* evidence of an offence, then we'll look into it exactly as we would any other allegation. Without fear or favour, and irrespective of how many complaints you make against me – and no matter to whom you send them!" Bryce told him.

Poole now sounded quite wretched. "What do you think I should do, then?"

"That's not for me to say, Minister. However, if you intend to deny everything, you could sue for libel – assuming we can find and unmask Nemesis. On the other hand, if you're charged with a criminal offence you'll need someone to look after you. Either way, it might be wise to consult a solicitor sooner rather than later."

Poole sighed. "I realise you won't give me details, but can you say if other people are receiving further accusations?"

"Oh, yes. In fact, of arguably more serious offences than the one laid at your door. Which brings us back to my original question: who could have known about these various matters? And, perhaps even more crucial – as the blackmailer seems to know that you spoke to the police despite his warning – who knew that you had done so?"

"I just can't think. As far as the original allegations are concerned, no one person; several were involved. But I spoke to nobody about contacting the police. I suppose various members of my staff saw you arrive the other day; perhaps someone recognised you and put two and two together."

Bryce felt he had had more than enough of the Minister. "We'll leave it at that for the moment, Mr Poole, but no doubt I'll be speaking to you again before long. Goodbye."

He quickly replaced his handset before Poole could say anything else. Although the politician hadn't said that the allegation was true, he hadn't denied it either. By denying receipt of the second letter, however, there was a clear implication that he had something to hide.

What hadn't been discussed was the matter of the threatened publicity. Bryce now gave this more thought. There were at least three ways in which the Minister's sordid business could reach the public: the blackmailer could inform the newspapers; the police could issue a press statement; Poole could pre-empt the situation and issue a statement of his own – either one of righteous denial, or one announcing his resignation.

Earlier, Bryce had seriously contemplated asking the papers to help in finding any other Nemesis blackmail victims, but that would inevitably have led to reporters ferreting around trying to pinpoint the existing ones. A second reason for not pursuing that course was there was no guarantee that other victims would come forward in answer to such an appeal.

No, the only time the police would be initiating publicity through the press was if, or when, someone was charged with an offence. And at present, it looked quite possible that the 'victims' might be charged before their blackmailer.

Bryce considered whether Poole would make any kind of statement himself and decided he wouldn't.

That left Nemesis. Given the stated intent to *'draw out the process of instilling fear'*, the DCS thought that the blackmailer would drag the thing out as long as possible. Perhaps a quiet tip to the Whips' office, for a start. Discreet enquiries would ensue. The Prime Minister would be informed. Poole's constituency chairman would hear about it. Then a letter to a newspaper – to *The Times*, or perhaps to the *News of the World*. The editors wouldn't publish anything immediately, but – certainly in the case of the *News* – reporters would investigate. Word would get around.

This was of course nothing more than a hypothesis, but Bryce thought it was a fair one. What he couldn't know was whether the blackmailer would start priming the newspapers before he provided the police with tangible evidence.

The telephone rang again. This time it was Charrington, who wasted no time on courtesies. "You won't like this, but I've decided to retract my complaint. I've had time to reflect and pray on the matter, as a man of my calling must. I regret that I didn't do that sooner. I'm convinced that Nemesis has some sort of mental affliction. It would be very wrong of me to pursue a vindictive course against a troubled soul, when forgiveness is my Christian duty. I intend to 'turn the other cheek', as scripture prescribes. I don't want you to look into the matter any further. I intend to forget the ludicrous allegations that were made against me, and you must do the same."

"Do you mean the allegations in the original letter, or the later allegations," asked Bryce, pointedly.

"Later allegations?" blustered the Prelate.

"Please don't prevaricate," replied the Chief Superintendent. "I've also been sent a letter by your blackmailer. He mentions, *inter alia*, two extremely serious matters from your past. I repeat, Bishop, extremely serious matters.

"I am to be supplied with names and further details very soon. He also says that you are 'off the hook' as far as money is concerned – he's simply out to ruin you."

"Oh Dear God!"

"You may indeed need His help," remarked Bryce, who wasn't religious himself, but had respect for those with faith, provided they weren't hypocrites.

"Keeping quiet about your latest correspondence won't help you, but it might help us to find out who is responsible. Be so good as to let me have the letter and envelope without delay. And any more which may arrive.

"By the way, I don't know if it was mentioned in your letter, but the writer seems to know that you, and others, contacted the police. Any idea how that could have leaked out?"

"No. Nobody knows, not even my Chaplain who in most matters is my closest confidant. Someone from the hotel, perhaps?"

"Unlikely. I didn't even give my real name, let alone the fact I was a policeman."

"A leak from Scotland Yard, then?"

"Since we have no idea who the blackmailer is, it's hard to see how the very few officers who are aware of the letters could have passed anything on. And they are all trustworthy, by the way, so it's far more likely to be someone at your end. Never mind. I expect you to contact me immediately if you hear anything further."

As before, after putting the telephone down Bryce reviewed the conversation. The Bishop, unlike the Minister, hadn't asked for suggestions as to what he should do. Nor, apart from a plea to the Almighty, had he given any indication of concern. But his other actions – in trying to withdraw his complaint, and in concealing news of the second letter from the police – made it crystal clear that the new allegation had some foundation.

The letters had already caused the deaths

of two people, and another was likely to be hanged. It now looked as though the outcome of this case would be disastrous for even more people. Whether the letter writer would be among them remained to be seen.

A few minutes before noon, Bryce opened a drawer in his desk and locked away all the sensitive documents. He then went downstairs to find Drummond. There was nobody apart from the DC in the general office, and Drummond sprang to attention as his boss arrived at the desk.

"Stand easy," said the DCS. I don't know if either Mr Haig or Kittow has explained this, but when you work with me there are two clearly-defined situations. One is the formal work situation, where you call me 'sir'. The other is when we are staying overnight on an away job – or like today when we're having a meal and not discussing work. Then, and only then, we relax the formalities. I call you by your first name, and you can call me Philip. Few people manage to do that, but 'guv' is easy enough for anyone. Just remember that when we leave the pub or wherever we are, we go back to work. Understand?"

"Yes, guv."

"Right – Alex tells me your name is Gerry. One other thing, I don't like drinking at lunchtime – one shandy or a half of bitter is okay, but we don't addle our brains so they don't work in the afternoon. Are you coming back to the Yard after lunch?"

Drummond confirmed that he still had another hour's work to finish. "There you are, then; I'm off home after this, but you're still on duty! Let's get down to the Albert."

Drummond was more than happy with this information, and delighted with the Albert. Both officers enjoyed a plate of sausages, mash, and gravy, washed down with a pint of shandy. The young detective was soon put at ease by the man five ranks his senior, and found himself telling some of his life story. Bryce passed on a few interesting items of general knowledge, but said nothing about himself.

To Drummond's relief, there was no mention of stations on the Piccadilly line extension.

***

At home in Greenford, Haig rarely spoke about the case he was working on, and the conversations during the weekend centred around Rosie, their outing that evening, and their tentative plans for moving home.

Fiona Haig was still overjoyed about her husband's new status. She had long expected that he would reach the rank of Inspector one day, but had assumed (like him) that it wouldn't happen for another four or five years. While believing implicitly in the merit of Alex's appointment, she knew that Mr Bryce must have been largely responsible for pushing it through. Unknown to her husband, she had drafted a letter of thanks, which she intended to send when she was satisfied with the wording.

In the Bryce house, Veronica was similarly comfortable with the fact that her husband deserved his promotion. Unlike Fiona Haig, she didn't think about it much more, simply taking it for granted that Philip would inevitably move to the top eventually. This promotion was a natural step in that progression.

The conversations in this household, from Saturday afternoon to breakfast on Monday, were wide-ranging. One topic, to which they returned several times, concerned the effect of the pregnancy on their way of life. That evening, the best part of two hours was spent on this important matter. They considered the best ways in which Veronica's business could continue, and moved a little closer to decisions regarding domestic help.

The other principal topic was the current blackmail case. Bryce had no hesitation in discussing cases with Veronica. She had been actively involved in helping him before, and he found it useful to have someone with insight and intelligence, outside the Met, with whom he could discuss facts and ideas. He outlined the situation to her.

"I haven't met Gerry Drummond, Philip,

but I can picture him from your description. Oh to be a fly on the wall at the bureau on Monday, and watch him trying to persuade them to find him a job as a junior footman or something that I imagine he knows absolutely nothing about!"

Bryce grinned. "To be honest, Vee, and assuming that this agency is indeed the centre of the blackmail web, I can almost admire the organisation here. The administrative effort just to set up the scheme must have been significant. But once set up, there's such a wide variety of allegations; against so many different people and over such a long period of time. Bearing in mind that much of what is passed on may not be immediately useful, the collation of all that disparate data must require either an administrative genius or a large team.

"I'm also exercised by how the author knew that at least three people had defied his instructions, and contacted the police."

"Maybe he didn't know," said Veronica. "Perhaps he just assumed that some of the recipients would do that. After all, everyone is always encouraged to report such things. Perhaps he even knew the character of some of his victims so well that he could be pretty sure about what they would do."

"That's true, I suppose."

Earlier in the week Bryce had impressed upon his Secretary the need for complete confidentiality, and had ordered transcripts to be made of all the letters, including the one to himself. He took these out of his briefcase and showed Veronica, drawing her attention to the adoption of 'Nemesis' as the blackmailer's pseudonym.

"Do you think we might conclude anything about the sex of the writer from the use of that word?"

Veronica read all the letters very carefully before sitting back and looking at her husband.

"As you said earlier, the author has a first-class grasp of written English. We can assume a highly educated person, who would likely be aware that in mythology Nemesis was female.

"However, surely such an intelligent individual would also have the wit to bluff, or even to double bluff?"

"Exactly the point Adam Kittow made, Vee."

"Same with the general wording," continued Veronica. "I don't know any woman who would write in that way – there's something distinctly masculine about it – but again, an intelligent woman might do so as a bluff.

"So, in answer to your question, no; I don't think you can draw any conclusion about sex. And Philip, if the allegations are true, I do hope you'll be able to get the proof. Hartley just sounds like a crook, albeit large-scale rather than petty. But the other two seem to have done things which are shocking and vile. They need to be properly punished."

"Yes, and if that's the case I shall use all of my ever-increasing power to see that happens, my angel," replied her husband.

CHAPTER 15

Monday 6th November, 1950

Just after nine o'clock, Detective Constable Drummond found the Coates Employment Bureau in Lower Regent Street. A number of cards advertising vacancies were displayed in the window, and he made a show of perusing these with interest before he pushed open the door.

Standing inside the agency, he was surprised to see the front area of the establishment was small, barely deep enough to fit four chairs on each of the two shorter walls.

These snug dimensions were explained by the partition wall which faced him as he entered – the premises had clearly been sub-divided. The DC saw a closed door and a closed hatch in this stud wall, the latter displaying a notice politely recommending '*Please Ring the Buzzer and Wait.*' The clacking of busy typewriters came from behind the wall as he reached for the button to comply.

The double doors of the hatch swung open revealing a shelf holding a small pile of preprinted forms, a pen, and an ink bottle, beyond which he saw a decent sized office. A pair of desks were pushed together in the centre of the room. Each held an Imperial typewriter, the sources of the sounds he had heard. A number of filing cabinets filled one wall, with a Gestetner Cyclograph duplicator also visible. The usual small office equipment of coat stand, sink unit, and tea making items took up the rest of the space.

A girl of about his own age stood facing him. She gave him a dimpled and very bright smile. Glossy auburn hair waved about her temples and shining blue eyes regarded him in a friendly manner as she enquired "Can I help you?"

Drummond looked back at her, and suddenly wished he didn't have to lie. She looked and sounded really lovely. If he'd met her anywhere else he'd have struck up a conversation and offered to take her somewhere for a drink. He felt sure he would then ask her if she fancied meeting up again another time – a trip to the cinema, perhaps, or to go dancing at The Palais.

Realising he was being examined by the pretty blue eyes he felt himself turning red, and embarked on the necessary tale. "I'm looking to get out of my job and into something completely different. I've decided I need a change."

"You've come to the right place, then," she said encouragingly and smiled again, her charm and appeal increasing by the second to the smitten young detective.

The girl picked up the pen and prepared to write on one of the forms. "Name and address first, please; then your date of birth. After that, I'll make a note of any qualifications, followed by what it is you do at the moment and what sort of work you're looking for."

Drummond was word perfect. He smoothly supplied his friend's ID particulars before telling her, "I work at Crossness. I started there straight from school, but I've had enough of it. I can't see myself progressing because it's an old pumping station – they'll be closing it before long."

This was perfectly true. His friend had told him he expected Crossness to be decommissioned in the not-too-distant future, and that was the main reason why he was considering leaving and following Drummond into an occupation which he foresaw could never close down, and would therefore be a job for life.

"I was hoping to work as indoor staff for some bigwig. I'm not picky about what I do."

He quickly added the point which the Chief Superintendent had made. "I'd have to learn the ropes from the bottom up, I suppose, being new to that sort of life. But I reckon it'd be an improvement on what I'm doing, and I'd like to give it a try."

Now thoroughly underway with his

deception, he told another lie. "A couple of my older relations were in service. My Mum says they were very happy. Both dead now, unfortunately, so they can't put in a good word for me, otherwise I'm sure I'd get fixed up quite easily."

The girl listened and wrote, then turned her eyes up at him again to ask, "So what did you do at Crossness pumping station? I don't think I've ever heard of it. Does it pump gas or water?"

"In a manner of speaking you could say a bit of both really," said Drummond, keeping a very straight face for the moment, and looking directly into the twin pools of beguiling blue. "It's a sewage pumping station."

The charming dimples reappeared, this time with a peal of laughter. The girl had a sense of humour, and he found himself liking her even more as he laughed with her.

Several minutes were spent recording Drummond's friend's very respectable range of skills. Dealing with the fact that he hadn't brought any references with him, he said he thought his manager at Crossness would oblige, and he could ask an old teacher if a second reference was required.

When the application sheet was completed the girl blotted it and told him, "All applications for service jobs are dealt with by the owner and her daughter. Their offices are upstairs. My colleague and I take everyone's details, but we only ever contact employers and prospective employees for the other vacancies we handle – gardeners, chauffeurs, factory workers, delivery drivers, and so on.

"If Mrs Wyatt likes you on paper, she'll call you upstairs." She lowered her voice. "There's a shortage of people of every description wanting to go into service – especially younger men who can drive and have mechanical knowledge, like you do. They're very sought after because they're handy as chauffeurs and for maintaining vehicles, as well as other duties.

"If you can wait, I'll take this to her right away." She blushed. "And I'll put in a good word for you at the same time. I'll tell Mrs Wyatt how politely you speak and how smartly turned out you are. It all helps."

"Oh I can stay all right!" Drummond thumbed over his shoulder at the waiting area. "I'll take a seat, shall I?" he asked, delighted at how well things were going. "And thank you!"

The girl nodded and smiled enchantingly at the young detective as she shut the hatch.

Not ten minutes later, a woman in her late twenties opened the door beside the hatch. Drummond, hoping to catch another glimpse of the girl he had admired, was disappointed. The door led into a narrow corridor with a flight of stairs straight ahead. The office behind the hatch clearly ran parallel with this corridor and staircase, but was partitioned off by yet another stud wall, and he could see that the door which connected the two areas was shut. He realised that unless the hatch was open when he left, he was unlikely to see the girl again.

At the top of the stairs he was shown into a smart office and introduced to Mrs Wyatt by his escort who, now he saw the older woman, was obviously the daughter mentioned downstairs. Leaving him with the bureau owner, a lady in her late fifties, Miss Wyatt left the room and closed the door behind her.

After the attractive and natural appearance of the girl downstairs, Drummond found the woman disconcerting. Her makeup was thickly spread over her face, but her eyebrows were plucked out of existence and replaced with a hard, brown, pencilled line, perfectly matched to the colour of her dyed hair. Looking at her mouth, Drummond couldn't decide if her carmine lipstick was deliberately over-applied, or whether she had accidentally gone beyond her thin and shapeless lips.

Mrs Wyatt's voice was educated, but her manner was brusque to the point of rude. "Sit," she said, pointing at the chair facing her desk, closely scrutinising the detective as he obeyed.

"It's always possible to find suitable posts for the right people. But I see you didn't bring any references with you – should I read anything into that?"

She gave the detective no time to answer

before saying, in a far more approachable voice, "As it happens, that needn't matter if you turn out to be the right sort of person. You should tell me straight away, though, if there's anything in your past that I ought to know about."

Drummond thought her tactic was a clever one. Her tone was now marginally more wheedling than accusatory, and he felt that any applicant who had a past that they wished to keep hidden would find themselves confessing their wrongdoing and throwing themselves upon her mercy to find them work. He had virtually no time to think about how he should respond in order to achieve the required outcome of a job offer, but decided his best approach at this point would be a combination of looking a little shifty while sounding just a little defensive.

He began by shrugging his shoulders. "Well, I'm not a complete angel. I might have done a bit of this and a bit of that, from time to time. But only in the way that us lads sometimes do. Never anything physical, if you take my meaning."

None of this was true of the friend whose identity he was using. That young man was as upright as he was himself, but the detective said what he felt was needed. He looked at Mrs Wyatt with what he hoped was a convincingly casual 'what of it?' expression. In the absence of any sort of response, he gave another shrug before adding, "I suppose you could say I allowed myself to be led by the wrong company, on occasion."

"Example?"

The unexpected question was snapped out at him by Mrs Wyatt, pencilled eyebrows raised and carmine mouth sardonic.

Drummond kept his head and stared impassively at her as he prepared his answer. In the process, and quite unwittingly, he managed to look as though he was considering whether it was safe for him to reveal self-incriminating information.

"It's possible," he said carefully, thinking that allusions to theft might be his best choice, "I might've picked up things that I later realised weren't mine; and then just forgot to return them."

Deciding he didn't want to run the risk of being caught out by another question, Drummond crossed his arms and assumed a slightly truculent tone. "Let's leave it at that, shall we?"

He held the woman's gaze and then smirked, realising there was no advantage in looking or sounding remorseful. If he was to succeed he felt he had to convey a mixture of willingness and fearlessness towards criminal conduct, together with a lack of conscience. Police experience had shown him that these were typical characteristics of crooks.

The bureau owner said nothing, her

powder-plastered face again inscrutable.

Concerned that he might have been too abrupt in his last remarks, and inadvertently given the woman cause to reject him, Drummond decided it wouldn't hurt to make clear that he was also clever in his activities. "But I've never been caught, ma'am, and I haven't got a record. Nothing like that." He uncrossed his arms and leaned forward, holding the bureau owner's gaze. "You won't find anything official against me anywhere. No one will."

Mrs Wyatt looked over her new applicant again, a small smile playing on the red strip of her mouth. "All right. I believe I may have something very suitable for you. I'll be in touch by the end of the week. Make your own way out."

Drummond returned down the stairs. Passing through the front waiting area, he realised he was absurdly pleased to see that the hatch was open, even though there was no one waiting for attention. He looked into the back office and saw the auburn-haired girl looking intently towards the hatch. Seeing him, she rushed from her desk.

Blushing for a second time, she again lowered her voice so her colleague couldn't hear. "Might you get a letter to come back?"

"Looks like it."

The pleasure on the girl's face was all the encouragement Drummond needed. "Can I see you again properly then? Take you out for a bit of lunch or something?" he asked quietly.

The young detective was soon sailing out of the poky little waiting room, revelling in the girl's shyly whispered:

"Yes, I'd like that. My name's Anna Berryman."

***

At ten-fifteen, Haig telephoned his boss to report that Drummond had returned from his task. The DCS told him to bring the team upstairs at once.

"Very interesting, and very well done," Bryce told Drummond, when the DC – without detailing his conversation with Miss Berryman – had finished describing his trip to the employment bureau.

The DCS gave the team the gist of his conversations with Poole and the Bishop.

"Two very unhappy men, then," remarked Haig.

"Indeed, but I can't pretend I'm sorry for them. We've a few more jobs to do now.

"Kittow, nip down to Records. Make sure they know you're working for me. Take the names of the various people we've heard about – all six victims, of course, plus Crossland, and those servants that we've got names for. See if we've got anything on any of them.

"Drummond, get on to Companies House. I want everything you can glean about Coates – names of the directors, and where they live. That's public domain information, so you shouldn't get any obstruction; if you do, give me a call.

"Inspector, I want you to draw up an outline plan for seeing as many of the servants – and Mrs Wyatt and her bureau staff – concurrently. For obvious reasons I don't want anyone tipping anyone else off. Even with all of us working separately we can only tackle them four at a time, so look to see if we can bring in a number of other officers. For any suspects outside London we can involve the local forces.

"Incidentally, gentlemen, there was nothing in the post this morning from Nemesis. Quite a disappointment; but maybe there'll be something in one of the later deliveries today."

When his men had left, Bryce settled down to his staffing task. He sketched out a staff tree, with job titles and provisional ranks. About half of the posts didn't have a name against them.

On a separate sheet of paper he listed eleven names, in two columns – five in one column and six in the other. The column of five names was headed 'out'.

He folded the larger sheet of paper, and placed both it and his list in an envelope. This he carefully locked in his desk drawer. Calling downstairs some time later, he invited Haig to join him for an early lunch. They walked up to Northumberland Avenue, and bought sandwiches and tea at the cabbies' shelter by

Embankment Place. A few yards away, they found a bench in Whitehall Gardens, and sat down to enjoy their lunch in the early November sunshine.

Several minutes were spent discussing the present case – both officers still perplexed as to how the letter writer had known that some of the recipients had contacted the police. Even if it was proved – as now seemed probable – that staff recruited through the bureau were involved, that couldn't explain how Nemesis knew that all three men had disobeyed instructions.

Bryce reported what Veronica had suggested, and explained why he still wasn't convinced. "The letter was pretty clear – '*I now learn that at least three of them did so*'. That doesn't suggest anticipation or guesswork – it implies that each of the three victims either had a spy very close to him – or all three had the same spy in common.

"Anyway, I want to have a chat about something else. This is entirely confidential. You're aware that I've been charged with reorganising the department – I gather there will be people looking into other departments, but I know nothing of that.

"I have some ideas as to how the department should be run in future. I've drawn up a rough plan – posts, ranks, and so on. Some posts have names pencilled in – yours for a start! There may be a small number of other promotions. And, most contentiously, I want to clear out a few useless bodies.

"What I'd like, entirely off the record, are your first thoughts about a few names.

"If I'm to continue as an operational detective, I shall need a deputy who is a proven administrator. I've reviewed the existing DCIs, and the only one I'd consider for that job is too valuable to take off the ordinary work."

Haig grinned. "I guess you mean Mr Weir, sir?"

"Yes. I've even considered a few uniformed chief inspectors, but it might be a step too far to make one of them effectively the second in command of the CID. So, I'm thinking of one of the existing experienced DIs. Any ideas?"

"I don't need to think very long, sir – Jack Nunn. If it's him you mean, he'd do a grand job, and have the respect of everyone else."

"Good – we're on the same wavelength. As for the dismissals I have in mind, I can think of five nominees from constable to chief inspector. I won't ask you to put names forward for that list, and it's by no means certain that I'll be able to get it approved anyway. But if I can, then openings arise for a few keener and more efficient replacements."

"I don't know if he's on your list, sir, and it may be a bit premature, but Kittow would be a deserving case to become detective sergeant," said Haig. "He's level-headed and dedicated, and performed well in the cases where he's supported us."

"He is indeed on my list. And I have two other names from outside the Met – men we've worked with ourselves. Any ideas?"

Haig thought for a second.

"Well, the two I'd suggest aren't very experienced, sir, but certainly showed great promise. Whether they'd want a transfer to the smoke is another matter. Lomax and Malan are the two I'm thinking of."

"Yes; the way Lomax performed in the witness box was impressive, especially as he'd never attended an Assizes before, let alone given evidence there. He might accept a job with us. Malan, on the other hand, has already been made up to sergeant, so I don't think the extra costs of living in London will be attractive to him, but I'd like to offer him the chance to transfer anyway.

Bryce made a ball of his greaseproof paper sandwich wrapping, and lobbed it neatly into a nearby bin. "Let's get back."

***

Back in his office, Bryce found his Secretary hovering.

"There's a letter arrived, sir – it's on your desk. Timmy Reeves brought it straight up."

"Thank you, Mrs Pickford. Please ask Inspector Haig to come up with the fingerprint gear."

Haig arrived, with Kittow and Drummond in tow. "The DCs have news, sir, so I brought them with me."

"Good. Kittow, you dust this new arrival," said Bryce, "whilst Drummond tells us what Companies House told him."

"Not a lot, sir. The directors are Mrs Beatrice Wyatt and Miss Maria Wyatt, both living at the same address in Erskine Hill, Hampstead. The registered office is the one I went to in Lower Regent Street.

"The company reported a loss in its first year, but after that it's produced a substantial profit."

Kittow looked up from his dusting. "Usual jumble of prints on this, sir," he said. "Posted yesterday afternoon in Mayfair. Shall I open it?"

Bryce nodded, passing over his paper knife and tweezers. Kittow carefully slit open the pale blue envelope and unfolded the letter inside. The spectators could see that this missive was much shorter than the last. The DC rapidly dusted both sides of the paper, and reported, as expected, that there was no sign of any prints. Glancing enquiringly at Bryce, his superior's nod told him he was to read the letter aloud, as he had before.

Dear Sir

I am moving against Poole first. I have written to two newspapers, the People and the News of the World, outlining his transgressions.

Given that both weeklies pride themselves on their investigative journalism, I confidently expect that reporters have already been deployed.

The Inspector who was bribed to close the rape case is Dennis Higgins, lately stationed in Poole's constituency. The man who bribed Poole is Leslie Fletcher, one of his constituents – it is his son, Edward, who should have been charged.

The girl is Joan Strachan. She is from a very poor background, and neither she nor her widowed mother ever stood a chance of being heard.

I have not informed Poole of this development, as I thought it would be far more amusing if the reporters arrive on his doorstep unexpectedly. Nor have I given him the details I have given you. I shouldn't put it past him to try a further bribe!

On the reverse of this letter are some useful addresses which, if you move quickly, will allow you to be ahead of the reporters.

Yours faithfully,
Nemesis

"As expected," said Bryce. "Just a minute, all of you." He picked up the telephone and spoke to the operator:

"If you get a reporter from either the *People* or the *News of the World* enquiring about anything at all, pass them on to me immediately. Make sure all your colleagues are aware of that."

He replaced the handset.

"What did you glean from Records, Kittow?"

"Several 'hits', sir. Galbraith's Crossland and Barratt's Saunders each have two previous convictions for theft from employers. Both served short terms of imprisonment.

"Couldn't find anything on the other servants, sir. But it's possible that provincial forces – in the Bishop's see and Poole's constituency – might have something.

"The other point is that Barratt himself had one conviction, for fraudulent conversion in March 1914. He got four years, so he probably sat out the Great War in prison."

"Not necessarily," said Bryce. "Prisoners and Borstal boys were often given the chance to join the army and go to fight, and thousands did. In one instance, a released burglar won the Victoria Cross, although he was later killed in action.

"The convictions for Aggie and the valet – I assume they were before being taken on by Barratt and Galbraith?"

"Yes, sir."

"Well, assuming the convictions weren't declared, we have to wonder if the Coates people just glossed over the absence of references – or supplied forged ones.

"Anyway, I suppose all that supports the notion that it's the domestic staff supplying at least some of the information. I'll call Putney and see if Galbraith is on remand in Wandsworth yet. Wherever he is, I'll get someone to go and ask him straight away whether he knew about Crossland's convictions – and whether he would have kept any reference that was supplied.

"Inspector, you and Kittow go down to Sussex now, and find this retired Inspector, Higgins. With a fair wind you should get to Lewes before three. I'll call ahead to tell the locals you'll be on their patch. The key thing is to get a statement. It'll be up to the locals to charge him, so don't arrest him unless he's difficult – although if Nemesis was correct in his first letter to us, Higgins will cooperate."

Haig was curious. "How does Nemesis know about Higgins? It doesn't seem likely that a police inspector would employ anyone from Coates or one of the longer established agencies they swallowed up."

"No, it doesn't seem likely in the ordinary way of things. But I suppose there are a number of possibilities. Higgins – or his wife – may have private means beyond his police income. An alternative explanation is that the information about Higgins came from whoever found out about Poole.

"Anyway, when you get something from Higgins, go and find this Leslie Fletcher. He's probably less likely to be cooperative, but assuming Higgins makes a statement, you can use that to exert a bit of pressure on Fletcher.

However, it's possible that Higgins can't actually give any direct evidence against the man, so if Fletcher won't give a statement, I don't think you have enough to arrest him on suspicion of bribery.

"Don't bother with the son and the poor girl; that's for the local boys. I hope they deal with it properly this time around. I'll submit a report to the Chief Constable without delay, as soon as we've got a statement or two; but our overarching concern is to get evidence against Poole.

"I'm abandoning the idea of trying to interview several of the servants simultaneously, by the way. It would stretch us too far – we just don't have the manpower. So, Drummond, while these two are dealing with our bent former inspector, when I've made my calls you and I will go and see if we can find Aggie Saunders and question her in one of the police stations in Whitechapel.

"Depending on what she tells us, and also on what Galbraith says, I'll see if I can justify asking for a search warrant for the Coates premises."

Haig and Kittow left. Drummond remained as instructed while the DCS made his calls. Neither of these took very long.

"We've spoken to Galbraith, sir," reported DI Haynes. "He's still being held here in the police station. He says there were no written references from previous employers, but it seems Mrs Wyatt telephoned him in support of Crossland. He is adamant that she stated the man was of good character."

"I suppose that's what we were expecting, Inspector. She was too canny to commit that to writing."

Bryce thanked the Putney DI, and rang off. "You probably heard that, Drummond – Crossland came with a 'good character' reference. Let's go and find Aggie Saunders."

CHAPTER 16

Haig and Kittow had agreed to split the driving, and tossed a coin to see who took the wheel for the outward journey to Sussex. Kittow called correctly.

They pulled up outside a large semi-detached bungalow, with an immaculate front garden. The man who answered the door bell looked nothing like a former senior policeman. Kittow thought he would have looked completely at home on a seafront, wearing a large white apron around his ample girth and selling ice cream from a barrow attached to a bicycle, or possibly whelks from a stall. In his mid-fifties, barely reaching the minimum height, he was almost bald. In other circumstances, both officers thought he would be a jovial character, (Pickwickian, even, thought Haig), but today his demeanour was glum.

After brief introductions on the step, he invited the Yard officers inside, where they politely refused his offer of coffee.

"Well, then," said the ex-Inspector in a

pleasant Sussex burr, "let's not be coy. I know exactly why you're here, and I'm only surprised it's taken so long.

"I'll tell you straight out – I was a stupid beggar. I took a bribe to turn a blind eye, and haven't slept well since. It was the one and only time it happened in over thirty years. I have no excuse beyond the fact that the pressure from Poole was intense. And I don't know if you're aware of this, but the lad's father is on the Police Watch Committee.

"The offer came just as my daughter and her family were saving to go to Australia on the assisted passage scheme. I gave them most of the money to help start their new life down under.

"Anyway, I've seen a solicitor, and drawn up a statement, which I've signed. No doubt I shall be prosecuted now, and maybe lose my police pension." He produced a single sheet of paper and handed it to Haig, who read it and passed it on to Kittow.

"Are you going to arrest me, Inspector?"

"No, Mr Higgins. For the moment we're only interested in other matters. It'll be up to Sussex to decide what action to take against you. I imagine they'll investigate the alleged rape now, though.

"There's one thing that's been puzzling all of us at the Yard, and that's how the allegations in every case relate to events from years ago – up to forty years ago, in one instance. Can you explain how your matter has only now been used against you, years after it happened?"

Higgins was morose. "No, I can't. A few weeks ago I received a letter signed Nemesis. The writer said he was aware of what had happened – he even gave the date – and that it would be better for me if I confessed before it was all made public. I didn't need much persuading; I've felt guilty about what happened to the girl ever since.

"The letter, which I've destroyed by the way, told me to place an advertisement in the Times personals stating: *'Nemesis, H agrees'*. I did that a couple of days later. That's over a week ago now, and I haven't heard anything since.

"I've racked my brains to think how this got out. Nobody knew about any of it except Poole, Fletcher, his son Edward, and me. But why should any of those three start squawking?"

Haig made a non-committal gesture, and stood up. He had no intention of sharing details of the investigation. Leaving the disgraced and disconsolate former inspector to his speculations, the Yard officers returned to their car and went in search of Fletcher, Higgins having confirmed that the address provided by Nemesis was correct.

"If the theory that domestic staff are gathering the information is right, one way this could have leaked out is if someone overheard a conversation – Poole talking either to Fletcher or to Higgins."

"Yes, sir, but I suppose that could have been either Poole's man or Fletcher's man."

"Aye. We'll see in a minute what Fletcher has in the way of a household and staff."

The house they arrived at was double fronted with three storeys and dormer windows set into its roof. It stood in an unusually wide street of similarly fine properties.

The bell was answered by a uniformed maid. Haig wished her "good morning," and explained the reason for their visit.

The girl looked unsure. "The master isn't in," she explained, "but he usually gets back at about half past four. I could ask the mistress if she'll see you?"

"If you would, please," replied Haig, giving her a card.

The detectives were shown into a parlour. Within two minutes, a sleekly coiffured woman swept in, a strong smell of lily of the valley arriving with her.

"Good afternoon, gentlemen," she said; "I'm Maureen Fletcher. Do sit down." Glancing at Haig's card in her hand she asked, "What can I do for you, Sergeant?"

"Actually that's a bit out of date, madam – it's Inspector now. As you see, we're from Scotland Yard. We need to speak to your husband."

"Scotland Yard – dear me! I imagine it's

something I can't possibly help you with!"

Haig agreed with a smile. "Most unlikely, madam. We'll wait for your husband, if we may."

"Of course; he should be back before long. Can I get you anything to eat or drink while you're waiting?"

Haig thanked her and declined.

"Make yourselves comfortable in here, then, and as soon as he arrives I'll send him through."

The two officers studiously avoided discussing anything to do with the case, and talked generalities. Haig remarked that he had once given evidence at Lewes Assizes, in the days before he had been allocated to Mr Bryce.

"Unusual town railway-wise – three different ways you can get to London, and three lines out the other way."

"Seems in this part of the world there were a lot of lines for a fairly rural area," said Kittow.

"True," replied the Inspector. "Even more so in your county next door." He gave a short discourse about the rivalry between the railway companies in south-east England, and how the policies of duplicating lines – nearly financially disastrous in the late 19th century – had proved invaluable in wartime.

Kittow was grinning from ear to ear as Haig finished his railway monologue. "Apart from your accent, sir, you're beginning to sound just like Mr Bryce," he said.

Before Haig could respond, voices could be heard in the entrance hall, and the detectives' heads swivelled towards the door. Moments later a man entered the room and Haig once again performed the introductions as he and Kittow rose to meet their host.

Fletcher told the officers to resume their seats and sat down himself as reciprocal assessments took place. The detectives observed a clean-shaven man in his fifties, dressed in a pinstripe three-piece suit with a fob chain across his waistcoat. Both officers were struck by his confident and self-satisfied air.

"Gentlemen, what can I do for you?" asked Fletcher. "Something to do with the Watch Committee, I take it?"

"No, sir," replied Haig. "Perhaps Mrs Fletcher didn't explain. We aren't local officers, we're from Scotland Yard."

Fletcher frowned. "I don't understand."

"We're investigating a matter of attempted blackmail. Do you know David Poole?"

"Yes, of course. A good chap – I've known him for years. He was our MP here long before he became a minister. Someone trying to blackmail him, are they? By Jove, the country's going to hell in a handcart these days!"

Fletcher stood up and tugged down sharply at his waistcoat. The gesture was an unmistakeable signal to the Yard detectives that they were being dismissed.

"Don't see how I can help you. I'll see you out."

"It's actually all a bit more complicated, sir," said Haig, deliberately pummelling the square squab behind him before sitting further back in his armchair and crossing his legs. "The attempted blackmail isn't only of Mr Poole. The threats extend to a number of other people."

Haig spoke with emphasis. "Evidence has emerged to suggest that the allegations contained in some of the blackmailer's letters are in fact true. As a result, our investigation has broadened in scope to cover these other very serious offences."

If Fletcher was concerned he didn't show it. Still standing, he tugged at his waistcoat again, and fiddled with one of his cufflinks. "What you seem to be saying is that David may have done something which he shouldn't, and someone has found out about it. I can't begin to fathom why Scotland Yard thinks that has anything to do with me!"

Haig was now blunt. "It's alleged that you bribed Mr Poole, so that he in turn could bribe a police officer. As a result, it's said that an investigation into an alleged offence by your son, Edward, was improperly closed down."

"Rubbish!" exclaimed Fletcher. "If I'd wanted to exert influence in something like that – which I didn't – why should I need to involve Poole?"

"Because as a member of the Watch Committee it wouldn't have looked good for you to approach a police officer direct, so you needed a catspaw," suggested Kittow, speaking for the first time.

Fletcher glowered down at him. "If anyone dares to repeat any of this in public – including you, young man – I shall sue!"

"Aye, well that's something you might do," replied Haig. "But then again, you might not when you learn that there's a witness. The police officer, whom the letter-writer said took the bribe, admits doing so. He's given us a formal statement to that effect."

Haig let this sink in before prompting Fletcher. "Would you like to make a statement yourself, under caution?"

Fletcher's response was instantaneous. "No! I need to speak to my solicitor." Passing a hand over his mouth he suddenly dropped back into his chair.

"Always a wise decision to take legal advice in these circumstances, sir," said Haig. "I can tell you that the Yard isn't directly concerned with your son. But as it's inevitable that his matter will be resurrected and thoroughly investigated, you might tell him to consult a solicitor, too."

Satisfied that Higgins had been correct in identifying Fletcher, Haig pressed for more.

"We have suspicions as to how the various bits of information have been acquired by the blackmailer, but as yet we have no proof. The allegation concerning you and Mr Poole must have leaked somehow. If you won't make a statement now, perhaps you'd like to co-operate and help us establish how that leak happened. Did you confide in anyone about this matter? Or do you have an employee who might have overheard a conversation between yourself and Mr Poole? We're tracing a number of such people in connection with our other enquiries."

Fletcher stared blankly for a moment, and then an expression of understanding passed over his face.

"I used to have…" he broke off. "No, I don't want to say any more now. If you aren't going to arrest me, please just go away." He stood again and gave his waistcoat a final tug, the gesture now a diminished and feeble attempt to assert his authority.

"We aren't going to arrest you, Mr Fletcher," said Haig, rising. "That'll be for the local police to action. I will just warn you that it would be very unwise to use your contacts to intervene on your behalf. I can tell you that the Chief Commissioner of the Met is involved personally; and if your Chief Constable hasn't been briefed about you yet, he will be very soon.

"Should you change your mind and decide to make a statement regarding your bribe to Mr Poole, contact me or Detective Chief Superintendent Bryce. The number is on the card

I gave your wife. Good afternoon."

As the detectives turned towards the door, Fletcher suddenly flapped his hands and motioned them to sit down again. He was clearly on the horns of a dilemma, and the Yard men watched and waited until he was ready to speak.

"It's no use; I shall have to tell you." It was as if the words were being dragged from him.

Haig immediately issued a formal caution, and Fletcher merely nodded.

"I have reason to believe that a man I used to employ made a habit of eavesdropping, and worse. In the end, I dismissed him after catching him looking through papers on my desk. His name is Roberts – Howard Roberts.

"He couldn't have heard the conversation between Poole and me, as you suggest, Inspector, because it didn't take place here. But what he almost certainly did hear was a conversation between my son and me. Actually, Roberts wouldn't have needed to strain his ears, as the conversation was carried on in fairly loud voices.

"Edward told me this girl had accused him, and had gone to the police. I told him he was an idiot for involving himself with a low-class trollop, and that I supposed I was going to have to sort things out.

"I can recall my next words pretty clearly: 'I can't intervene directly. I'll talk to David Poole. He's not averse to buying what he wants. I'll pay him, and he'll sort out the local police inspector.'

"So that's what happened. I'm not proud of what I did, but one's children…"

"This man Roberts, sir – did he by any chance come via an agency called Coates in London?"

"No, I've never heard of them. He came through Napier's."

"Let's have a statement," said Haig, fully aware that Napier's was one of the agencies taken over by Coates.

It took less than twenty minutes for Fletcher to write and sign the statement, which dovetailed perfectly with Higgins' own. This done, Fletcher querulously asked what would happen next.

"That I can't say. If Mr Poole is charged with an offence, then it's certain you would be called as a witness – unless he admits it, of course. But Scotland Yard isn't concerned with any offences which you, your son, or Higgins might have committed. Those are entirely a matter for the local constabulary.

"It's up to you, of course, but I would suggest that your continued presence on the Watch Committee isn't appropriate."

The detectives again stood to leave. "And I strongly urge you not to contact Mr Poole," said Haig as they showed themselves out of the room.

Kittow grinned as he climbed into the passenger seat of the car.

"Nice one, sir – especially mentioning the

Commissioner. For the second time in half an hour I thought I was listening to the Chief Super again."

"Aye," laughed the Inspector. "I've learned a lot from the boss. I'm nowhere near as clever, or as knowledgeable, but I can follow his style. In there I just thought Fletcher needed a bit of a deterrent to make him think twice before trying to talk to any police officer again, with a view to getting more blind eyes turned. But then he caved in anyway.

"Right," he continued as he started the Wolseley's engine. "The first place we need to find is a decent roadside café where we can get something to eat, and a telephone so I can report to Mr Bryce."

CHAPTER 17

While half of the team was cruising towards leafy Sussex, the other half was driving through the East End of London with Bryce at the wheel. Drummond didn't know whether to be pleased or disappointed that his new boss made no attempt to ask him difficult questions about architecture during the journey, and indeed hardly spoke a word.

The Constable was impressed by the fact that the DCS took the car to their destination without asking him to consult a street map. When they stopped outside the address given for Aggie Saunders, he queried this.

"Have you done 'the knowledge' sir?"

Bryce laughed. "Nothing so complicated. It might look as though I used to be a cabby, but in fact I was stationed in this division for nearly two years, as a DI. I had to come here once or twice, and I remembered it."

Both sides of the street were composed of terraced homes, all built with the once yellow, but now smog-blackened, London brick. The continuity of the terraces was broken wherever wartime bombs had fallen, and the resultant gaps in the otherwise uniform housing were sad reminders of the pounding the area had taken during the blitz.

There were no front gardens, the stone doorstep of each house abutting the pavement. The doorstep of the house they approached was freshly scrubbed, with the curtains in the small front window neatly tied back behind sparkling clean panes of glass. Someone clearly took pride in the upkeep of this home.

Drummond gave the shining brass knocker a good bang. A woman who might have been any age between sixty and eighty opened the door. Cigarette in mouth, she glared at them.

"Whatever yer sellin' I don't want none," she announced and prepared to close the door. Drummond was a fraction quicker, and stuck his boot over the threshold.

"Police," he said, showing his warrant card. The woman opened the door wider.

"We need to see Aggie Saunders," explained Bryce.

"She's not 'ere; she's dahn the fishmonger's. What's the little baggage done nah, then?"

With longer to look at the woman, each officer realised that she was actually much younger than his first estimation.

"Probably nothing that'll get her another term in prison," said Bryce, his manner as relaxed as if he were having a garden fence discussion with the woman about the price of the fish the girl was fetching. "But she may have important information about a very serious matter."

"Stoopid little tart!" came the sharp retort. "In an' aht o' trouble, that one! Well, it's only a 'undred yards dahn the road and rahnd the corner. She's wearing a green coat and carryin' a string bag. You want 'er; you go find 'er."

With that, the woman pointedly looked down at Drummond's boot. "I'd be obliged if you'd take your hoof aht of my door-'ole." As soon as Drummond complied she slammed the door.

Bryce smiled at the DC. "Most likely as honest as the day is long, herself, and at her wits' end about her daughter."

He looked past Drummond. "As it happens, I've a feeling we're in luck. This looks like our Aggie coming along now."

A tall girl in a green coat rounded the corner of the road. Swinging a bag with a newspaper wrapped parcel showing through its diamond mesh, she walked towards them and stopped outside the house, eying the two detectives standing by the car.

"You're busies," she said, accusingly. "An' I ain't done nuffink."

"Maybe you have, maybe you haven't," said Bryce. "Give the fish to your mother while it's nice and fresh, Aggie, and we'll go and have a chat in Leman Street."

For a moment the girl looked as though she would drop the bag and run, but then changed her mind and opened the door. Putting the bag down on the linoleum inside, she shouted something to her mother.

"Let's go," she said, climbing unbidden into the back seat of the Wolseley as though in the habit of being squired around London by the police. Drummond wasn't sure whether to join her, but Bryce, smiling, indicated he should get in the front.

Aggie didn't have much time to enjoy her ride, as the police station was less than five minutes away.

Inside, Bryce was immediately greeted with a warm and surprised "Hello, sir! Long time since we've seen you in here!" from the Custody Sergeant.

"Nice to see you again, Sawyer," smiled Bryce, "and I'm glad to see you've got your stripes – well done." He nodded at Aggie, "We need to borrow an interview room for a while. Can you manage that for us?"

"'Course, sir. Number two's free; you know where to find it. I'll fix up a brew for you all."

The three sat down in the bleak little room, and looked at one another. The girl was perhaps in her late twenties, slim, with stiff, permanently waved, dark hair. She was not unattractive, but rather hard-faced, her choice of hairstyle not helping to soften her features.

"Well, Aggie, let me introduce us. I'm Detective Chief Superintendent Bryce, and this is Detective Constable Drummond. We aren't from the local police division, we're from Scotland Yard."

The girl looked at him warily. "A Chief Super? Never 'ad no one 'igher than a sergeant on me back before. And from the Yard, no less." She gave a sneer, "Am I supposed to be impressed, or wot?"

Bryce ignored her irrelevant question. "Until very recently you worked for Julian Barratt, in Tonbridge, yes?"

"'Sright. He let me an' the cook go. Said he was goin' away." She sniffed and inspected her fingernails. "'Salright for some, innit? Up an' away somewhere nice whenever they feel like it."

Bryce also ignored the grumble. "Were you employed through Coates?"

The girl looked at him. The officers could see that she was trying to work out where this line of questioning was going.

"If it helps, Aggie, I'm not intending to charge you with an offence. It's not the likes of you we're after – as you must have realised when you remarked on my rank."

"I have to trust you then, is that it?" She considered her own question. "Orright then, I will. And yeah, I went through Coates. What of it?"

"I think you know the answer to that, Aggie. Your job wasn't just to work for Mr Barratt. It was to pass on gossip – and preferably anything more than gossip – that you picked up in your work, wasn't it? The juicier the better. Correct?"

Aggie's face altered. "And you reckon you really ain't after me?" She laughed sarcastically. "Only problem for you is that I ain't daft." As she spoke she pushed back her chair and stood behind it, her hands resting on the top rail, the mocking expression on her face matching her tone.

Bryce remained seated, looking up at her. "No, I'm really not after you, Aggie. When Mr Barratt told you he was 'going away', what he actually meant was he was going to kill himself. That's what he did a few hours after you and Mrs Marwick left. Driven to it by a blackmailer."

"Cor," muttered Aggie, "fancy that." She remained standing, but both detectives noticed that her grip on the chair tightened.

"There's more," said Bryce. "The same day, someone else shot his valet dead, believing the man had passed on some secrets." The Chief Super's tone was its most affable as he prodded at the weak spot in the woman's defences. "Just think Aggie, if Mr Barratt hadn't chosen to shoot himself, he might have shot you instead – like the other man who shot his servant."

Unsteady hands pulled back the chair and

Aggie sat down again with a thump, her eyes wide open and staring at the DCS. A uniformed constable arrived with a tray of tea.

When the cups were sorted out and the officer had left the room, the girl spoke first.

"So you're after this blackmailer then, is all?"

"That's right. Although it now seems that some of those being blackmailed may also be guilty of very serious crimes themselves. Even worse things than Mr Barratt did, perhaps."

Aggie examined the DCS carefully. She switched her gaze to Drummond, and then back to Bryce, after which her mind was clearly made up. Her evidence came quickly.

"Yeah, I was told to pass on anything and everything I learned about what Mr Barratt was doing, or had done in the past. I had to listen to conversations, and nose through papers and so on when 'e was out."

"Who gave you that instruction?"

"Mrs Wyatt, the agency boss."

"How were you rewarded?"

"Depends. Nothing mostly. But for a good bit, I'd get sent a postal order – a couple of pounds or more. When I dug out what 'e'd been doin' years ago before the first war, I got a cock 'n' 'en."

"How did you learn about that old matter, Aggie?"

"'E 'ad chats with some geezer on the dog 'n' bone. Four or five that I over'eard. 'Course, I could only get the one side, but enough to know 'e was feeling really bad about what they done together years ago.

"After I'd passed that on I was told to go through 'is desk. Did that a day or two later. Found a sort of letter; well, more a confession, really. Had lawyer's stamps all over it to say it's genuine. So I copied it all down – took me ages that did – and called them. Told me to put it in the post. Couple of days later I got a postal order for a pony. Best day's work I ever done. That was a few days before I got laid off."

"Who did you have to call when you had information?"

"A special number, different to the usual one. Only Mrs Wyatt or 'er daughter ever answered it; never the girls downstairs. For the post, I 'ad to write 'Private for Mrs Wyatt' on it in big letters."

"Good, Aggie, you've been very helpful." Bryce was satisfied that he had heard the truth.

"You know the drill. All we need now is a statement from you; then you're free to go. As long as you don't go talking to anyone from Coates, I won't charge you, but eventually you may have to give evidence against someone else. If I were you I'd find another agency."

Drummond, silent throughout, and shocked at the casual attitude Aggie had displayed towards her breaches of trust, suddenly heard his own voice chastising her.

"And if you've got the brains you were born with, you'll know you've got off dead lucky this time. Which won't be the case if we find out you've repeated your snooping sideline anywhere else!"

***

As on the outward journey, Bryce barely spoke on the way back to the Yard, but even Drummond, who hardly knew him, could see he was happy, and realised his boss didn't think he'd spoken out of turn to Aggie.

CHAPTER 18

Back in his office, Bryce drafted his report of events to date. This completed, he filled out an 'information', and a search warrant to go with it. These two documents were the essential paperwork which a magistrate would carefully consider before giving the necessary authority for a raid on the Coates bureau and the Wyatts' house. Although he had no intention of raiding the premises until the following day at the earliest, Bryce always prepared his paperwork well in advance, whenever possible.

He had just replaced the cap on his fountain pen when Reeves arrived from the post room.

"Another 'billy-doo' for you, sir," said the cheeky teenager.

Bryce glared at him, but after a second couldn't help grinning along with the boy. "The more the merrier, Reeves. As soon as you get them downstairs, I want them up here on my desk."

The youngster gave a small salute, clicked

his heels in acknowledgement, and was gone.

Bryce decided not to wait for someone to dust for fingerprints. The postmark on this one was a bit smudged, and he couldn't read the time, but it appeared to have been posted in Kensington. He slit open the envelope, carefully drew the letter out with tweezers, and read the contents twice.

He sighed, and decided to leave the letter for the time being. Picking up his external telephone, he asked the Yard operator to get him Bow Street court. Once connected, he identified himself, and requested an appointment to see the Chief Metropolitan Magistrate, but not in open court. This was arranged for five-thirty.

At five o'clock, the DCS left his office and jumped on a convenient tram for the ride along Victoria Embankment and through the Kingsway tunnel. Alighting at the Aldwych subterranean tram station, he had only a very short walk to Bow Street.

The Courts had already risen for the day, and Bryce was quickly escorted to the Magistrate's room.

"Afternoon, Chief Superintendent, or Philip – depending on whether it's business or pleasure today" said Clive Hudson, the Stipendiary Magistrate.

"Business, I'm afraid," replied Bryce with a smile.

"Let's get that out of the way first, then.

As you see, I've already heard that you've had yet another deserved promotion. I conclude that a man of your rank wouldn't come to me in this court if the matter wasn't delicate, because you'd send a subordinate to find a beak in Westminster. So what is it you think I can do for you?"

"Two separate requests, really, Clive. First I'm asking for search warrants for a business address and an associated residence. Perhaps we could take that matter first?"

Hudson nodded.

Very familiar with the routine, Bryce stood and picked up the New Testament which was lying on the table in front of him.

"I swear by Almighty God that the contents of this my information are true to the best of my knowledge and belief."

He formally identified himself, and then read aloud the words on the formal 'information' which he had drafted earlier, finishing by stating, "I want to search the agency offices, and also the property where the owner and her daughter reside."

The Stipe asked a few pertinent questions, before agreeing to issue both search warrants. He told Bryce to sit down again while he signed the various documents.

His pen recapped, Hudson looked at his visitor expectantly. "None of that seems at all controversial. What else are you after?"

The DCS outlined the whole case – the

blackmail letters, the murder and suicide, and the nature of the serious offences which had subsequently emerged.

"I intend to bring Lord Hartley in for questioning, but frankly the criminal aspect of his case is so old that I rather doubt whether there will be much chance of ever charging him.

"We haven't interviewed the witnesses against the Bishop – but if even one witness comes up to proof there will be enough to charge him.

"It's David Poole that I've come to you about. We have two competent witnesses who have made formal statements. I have another information here, ready for me to swear. What I'm after is a warrant for his arrest on two charges. The first is one of perverting the course of justice contrary to the Common Law, and the second under Section One of the Public Bodies Corrupt Practices Act."

Bryce, still under oath, read aloud his second information, and signed it.

The Stipe considered the fresh matter laid before him, looking reflectively at the detective. "You're relying solely on the matter of Poole shutting down the police investigation," he said. "I can't see that anything else is criminal."

He asked some more questions.

"What you're really getting at, Philip," the stipe said at last, with a half-smile on his face, "is that arresting a Minister of the Crown is a very big step – and you want me to take the responsibility off you!"

"I can't deny that, Clive," smiled Bryce. "But I do have the evidence."

"Very well, I'll issue the warrant."

These fresh papers signed, Hudson leaned back.

"Now, young man, you're obviously going places in your chosen field. But ten or fifteen years ago when we were briefly in chambers together, it was confidently expected that you'd rise to the top at the bar. If you'd stayed, a year or two from now you'd probably be getting a silk gown, and then who knows? Mine isn't a bad job; but by all accounts you could have done even better. Appointment as a red judge in your forties – that's what I heard predicted for you."

Bryce shook his head in amusement. "It's extraordinary how many people say those sorts of things to me now. I don't remember any such encouragement when I was sent out to do some boring County Court case, or mitigating a minor misdemeanour in a Magistrates' Court!"

The Chief Super spent a pleasant ten minutes chatting with his old colleague, before returning to Scotland Yard.

There, he sought out an Inspector in the uniformed branch, and arranged to borrow two cars, plus four male and two female officers for a job the following morning. His colleague raised his eyebrows when the DCS told him to have all six dressed in nondescript plain clothes.

"Not scruffy, but not Sunday best. I don't want to cause a stir in the street when we carry out this operation, so your people can consider themselves in the CID for the day."

As he re-entered his office, the telephone was ringing. The caller was Inspector Haig, who gave his report.

"Statement from Higgins, sir; full admission. Same for Fletcher. The likely leak was one of Fletcher's servants, who was later dismissed. The man was engaged through Napier's – one of the agencies swallowed up by Coates."

"Excellent! Couldn't be better!" said Bryce. "You can see how the Wyatt pair could have roped the former Napier recruits into their Coates blackmail clique. Simplest thing in the world to make contact with the staff from the other agencies with a 'pop in and see us to discuss your advancement' type of invitation. All they had to do was interview them, and sort out the ones inclined to corruption.

"It remains to be seen if we can bring charges against Fletcher. I don't condone what he did, but I probably wouldn't prosecute him myself, because I take the view that although offering a bribe is reprehensible, accepting it is the actionable offence. Poole is therefore the one in my sights. Higgins must definitely be charged; an example has to be made of a serving officer accepting a bribe – especially with regard to the case which he suppressed. The fact that he subsequently retired is irrelevant. As for Fletcher's son, if there's any evidence he can take everything that's coming to him.

"Anyway, well done; get back now, and the two of you go straight home. We have another letter from Nemesis, by the way, but we'll discuss that in the morning."

CHAPTER 19

Tuesday 7th November, 1950

The team assembled in Bryce's room at eight-thirty. The DCS had taken out the folder containing the latest letter, and was still staring at it blankly when his team arrived.

"You first, Inspector. You gave me an outline last night, but just expand a bit on what you and Kittow got."

Haig produced Higgins' and Fletcher's written statements, and gave a succinct report on the two interviews.

Bryce looked at Drummond. "Your turn, Constable; tell these two what we learned from Aggie yesterday."

The young detective gave an accurate account of the key points and was pleased to receive an appreciative "Well done" from the Chief Superintendent.

With everyone now up to date, Bryce opened the folder into which he had put the latest letter from Nemesis and said, "I've received a third communication from our correspondent

– the second in one day. I'll give you a break this time, Kittow, and read it to you myself.

Dear Sir

How are you getting on with Poole? Surely I've given you enough to charge him now?

I confess I'm getting impatient, so let's move on to the ignoble lords, temporal and spiritual.

First, Hartley. His earliest partner in crime was, as you have no doubt gathered, Julian Barratt. At the time, a few years before the Great War, Barratt was 'of good character' – or rather he was cunning enough to avoid getting criminal convictions. In fact, he was thoroughly crooked even at that young age. Whether the long firm fraud idea was his or Hartley's, I don't know. He says it was Hartley's, but they were both clever, and equally immoral.

They got away with at least three such frauds, and then had the brains to quit that field while they were ahead. Hartley went on to equally immoral but apparently legal schemes to make his huge fortune. Barratt also changed course, but stayed with a different kind of larceny, for which he ended up at the Old Bailey. Had he not pleaded guilty he might have been given six or seven years rather than the four he got away with.

I am sorry to learn that Barratt is dead. I had him earmarked as a witness against Hartley. I realise that it may not be possible to convict Hartley now – perhaps there's not even enough to bring him to trial.

I'm sure you have enough to arrest him, though, and give him a thoroughly uncomfortable time. One can only hope that the adverse publicity will be sufficient to finish him.

Second, Charrington. There is a variety of pear found in Gloucestershire called 'Stinking Bishop'. An excellent soubriquet for this repugnant man.

The names of two of those he abused whilst a vicar in Dorset are Mark Rhodes, now living in Blandford Forum, and Frank Porterfield now believed to be living in Shaftesbury. I'm sure you can find them without difficulty.

By the way, I've primed the press about their lordships. I look forward to hearing of Poole's arrest very shortly.

Yours, etc.,
Nemesis

Bryce looked up, and caught each officer's eye in turn. "Thoughts, gentlemen?"

"Time for a raid on the Coates offices, sir?" asked Kittow.

"Yes, within the next hour. I've already been granted warrants to search both the offices and the house.

"I forgot to ask – Fletcher's man; did you get his name?"

"Yes, sir, it's Howard Roberts."

"We need to interview him. Same terms

as for Aggie Saunders; we won't prosecute him if he co-operates. But we can hardly call Coates and ask where he can be found. So we'll have to get his details from their records during the raid, when we're getting the details for other servants in all the various households.

"We'll tackle the bureau first, and then we need to turn our attention to Dorset. Inspector, I want you and Kittow to go down there in the morning. As Nemesis hasn't been kind enough to provide addresses to go with the names, that'll be the next job.

"This afternoon, you'll need to spend some time on the telephone. Contact Dorset constabulary. I don't know the set-up down there. It's just possible that the headquarters will have a copy of all the electoral rolls for the county. Or you may need to consult the police stations in the towns mentioned. We want addresses for both these men, and it would make it a lot easier if you can get those before you leave. Might even be possible to make contact by telephone – they probably aren't on the telephone themselves, but when you've got the addresses you might be able to persuade the local police to pay them a visit and let them call from a police station to make appointments.

"The names aren't uncommon, so during your trawl you may find others. You'll have to filter those somehow to find the relevant ones, but remember the names could include the parents – and we certainly want to speak to them too.

"Right – let's get back to this morning. Kittow, I want you to take Drummond, and search the Wyatts' house. Go over all areas where there are any papers – and do it with the finest of fine-tooth combs. Bring away anything which looks even slightly relevant. If either Mrs or Miss Wyatt happen to be there rather than at their office, arrest them on suspicion of conspiracy to commit blackmail, and take them to West End Central. Understand?"

"Yes, sir," replied Kittow, pleased to be given this responsibility.

Drummond, on the other hand, wished he was going back to the agency. He wondered how Anna Berryman would react to the raid and her inevitable questioning, and found himself fervently hoping he would get a chance to see her again, another time.

"You and I will go to Lower Regent Street, Inspector," said Bryce. "We don't have spare DCs, so I've borrowed six officers from the uniformed branch, and put them into civvies for today. Two are female officers; they'll stay to answer the Wyatt's special telephone. We'll get them up here now."

He called to his Secretary to ask the two waiting WPCs to come upstairs.

As soon as the women arrived in his office Bryce explained some of the background to them, and then briefed them.

"If someone rings on the 'special line', you say you're authorised to take messages for Mrs Wyatt. Get as much information as you can: the caller's name, where he or she is working, and whatever it was they wanted to pass on about their employer.

"It may be that nobody will call, of course, but we have to be prepared. You'll both travel with me and Inspector Haig, and when we've gone you'll stay behind. Consider yourselves on duty at the bureau until close of business the day after tomorrow at least."

The older of the two WPCs, Vera Kibble, had a query. "Are we to stay all night, sir?"

Bryce realised his instruction had been unclear on the point and apologised, adding, "No, keep Coates' office hours. Go home this evening and return first thing tomorrow morning; plain clothes again. I'll post someone to watch the premises overnight. You can take turns to pop out during business hours."

The rest of the temporary team members waiting in the foyer received their instructions without any background detail. Bryce simply explained that it was hoped to question two women and arrest two others, and that the arrested women were to be conveyed in separate cars. They were not to be allowed within sight or sound of one another at any time.

"I'll arrest them," said Bryce, "assuming

they're there. You just escort them off the premises, take them to West End Central, and see them into separate cells. My Secretary will make sure the Custody Sergeant there is prepared.

"Let's go."

***

A few minutes later, four unmarked cars left the Yard and travelled in convoy along Whitehall, through Trafalgar Square, into Cockspur Street, and pulled up in Lower Regent Street.

The eight officers piled through the front door of Coates, the DCS leading. Aware of the office's layout from Drummond's description, he charged straight through the stud wall door and up the stairs with Haig, two of the constables just behind them.

The remaining four officers followed, but instead of taking the stairs they opened the door into the back office.

The two girls sat looking stunned as various men and women arrived beside their desks.

"Police," announced WPC Kibble. "We have a warrant to search the premises. Just stay where you are for the moment, until the Chief Superintendent comes downstairs. Are there any more of you in the building?"

No dimples were on display as Anna Berryman shook her head, her blue eyes huge and anxious. "Not down here. Mrs and Miss

Wyatt are upstairs, but there's a client in the employers' waiting room. She's come to see if we can find her a cook. It's the room on the right at the top of the stairs."

"Molly, you'd best go and stay with the lady," WPC Kibble told her colleague. "Don't let her leave until the Chief says so."

Meanwhile, Bryce and Haig were only seconds behind the downstairs action. Drummond's description of the layout had been very precise, but in fact the first two doors on the left were respectively labelled 'Mrs Beatrice Wyatt' and 'Miss Maria Wyatt'.

Bryce went into the first door without knocking. Mrs Wyatt, hearing the pounding of running feet on the stairs, had only enough time to rise from her chair before the Chief Superintendent and one of the constables were confronting her.

"Explain this outrage at once!" she demanded from behind her desk.

"Certainly," replied Bryce. "I am arresting you on suspicion of conspiracy to demand money with menaces. I warn you that although you are not obliged to say anything, whatever you do say will be taken down and may be used in evidence. Officers will take you to West End Central police station. I'll come and talk to you later."

The DCS produced his paperwork. "I have a warrant to search these premises and also your home. I'll begin by looking through your handbag and taking your keys."

Bryce curtly signalled to Mrs Wyatt that she should move away from her desk so he could take her place. He found a brown leather handbag on the floor beside the woman's chair. Undoing the clasp he shook the contents out onto the desk, and retrieved two bunches of keys.

Inspector Haig poked his head around the door.

"I've arrested Miss Wyatt, sir. She said nothing after caution. Shall I get her packed off to the nick?"

"Yes, please do; then send Constable Locke up here. We'll keep Mrs Wyatt with us and take her when we leave."

Haig nodded. "There's a lady in the upstairs waiting room, sir. An employer, apparently. WPC Carstairs is in there, keeping her company. What do you want done with her?"

"Send Carstairs in here to me, then check the lady's ID and take her name and address. Tell her that Mrs Wyatt sends her apologies, but is too busy to see her today. If she cares to telephone tomorrow, there may be more information."

Haig withdrew his head and shut the door.

Mrs Wyatt glared at Bryce and sneered. "Like she'll want to come back tomorrow when she's seen you lot crawling all over the place today!"

The Chief Superintendent ignored her.

Mrs Wyatt raised her voice at him. "I'll have you know that's my bread and butter you're sending away! You're killing my business and I shall have you for it – you can depend on that!"

Bryce gave no indication that he had heard a word the woman said, and issued his instructions to the two constables when they arrived.

"Locke, Miss Wyatt has already been removed from the next room. Take Mrs Wyatt in there now, whilst the Inspector and I search in here. Make sure she sits nicely and touches nothing at all, and above all, speaks to no one – apart from you, that is. She might want to give you a confession."

Constable Locke, well-built and very tall even when wearing a flat cap rather than a helmet, loomed over Mrs Wyatt as he escorted her next door.

"Carstairs, you can start running things upstairs now," said Bryce, and was pleased to see that the WPC was behind the desk and organising paper and pencils in readiness for any messages even before he had left the room. He passed over the two sets of keys from Mrs Wyatt's handbag. "Before you get settled, though, just nip downstairs and see which of these bunches of keys are for these premises – the other will hopefully be for the house."

He ran down the stairs and went into the office where the two girls were now looking less shocked, but still very unhappy.

"What's this all about?" asked Anna Berryman's colleague. "This lady won't tell us anything."

"No she won't – on my instructions," said Bryce. He explained the suspicion that the premises were being used for unlawful purposes. "Your employer and her daughter are under arrest. If you two didn't know what was going on, then you have nothing to worry about. If, on the other hand, you've been involved in that criminal activity, now's your chance to say so."

Bryce's tone was rather hard, and he watched the two girls closely as he spoke. Based on what Drummond had said about the domestic employment aspects of the bureau being dealt with exclusively by the Wyatts, he doubted if either of the downstairs staff knew anything. However, until proved otherwise he was fully justified in assuming the girls might both be connected to the Wyatts' enterprise in some way. Even if not as heavily involved, one or both might nevertheless be playing some part in the blackmail.

"But it's just an employment bureau," said Anna Berryman plaintively, sounding completely lost as to what was happening around her, "and it's been doing really well in the last year or two."

Her colleague's wordless and wide-eyed nodding to this statement went a long way to persuading Bryce that the two girls were ignorant of the agency's illegal sideline. "I know it has," he replied, reverting to his usual pleasant manner. "Unfortunately, we believe there was another activity going on, and it's less socially beneficial.

"I don't know what will happen to the bureau. But I want you both to stay here for the moment and carry on as near to normal as you can. Later, probably tomorrow, you'll each need to make statements. By that time things should be clearer."

WPC Carstairs came into the room, and reported that she had sorted out the office keys.

"Right – you hang onto those, Kibble," he told the WPC who had been watching over the two girls. "Lock the place up when you leave tonight. I'll take the rest. You and Carstairs settle in upstairs." He turned back to the two clerks.

"Tell me how telephone calls are made and taken. There are two incoming lines, yes?"

"That's right," said Anna. "One comes in here to our little switchboard," she pointed at the small Bakelite box on her desk. "We can either deal with those calls ourselves, or put them through to Mrs Wyatt or Miss Maria. The other line doesn't come in here at all; it only rings upstairs."

"What about visitors? And I don't mean potential employers like the lady who was upstairs when we arrived; I mean staff who already have a post. Does anyone like that ever come here?"

The second girl spoke again. "Oh yes, quite often. But we don't know why. They just give their names and ask to see one of the Wyatts. They always get to see them even if they haven't made an appointment."

"Very interesting – thank you. Between you, make a list, please, of all the names in that category of visitor that you can think of.

"When you've done that, you can answer the telephone, take details of all callers and visitors, or whatever else you normally do.

"WPC Kibble or her colleague will be in Mrs Wyatt's office for a couple of days. They'll take any calls on the private line. But if one of these unexpected visitors comes in, you're to alert the policewomen upstairs – exactly as you would have done for Mrs Wyatt – then let them go up as normal."

Bryce returned to Mrs Wyatt's office, where he found Haig going through the owner's desk.

"Nothing here, sir, as far as I can see." He pointed to the wall opposite. "Those big filing cabinets may hold something useful, though."

Bryce looked doubtful. "Assuming a high proportion of the servants placed by the bureau are perfectly honest, I'll bet it's their records which are stored up here. And I'm absolutely certain that there'll be no records of any extracurricular payments.

"Are there any filing cabinets next door?"

"No; it's the same size as this, but only the desk and some easy chairs."

"Right. We have to keep going through the motions. Find a removals firm and get all the filing cabinets to the Yard as soon as possible. Have an officer supervise the work and then travel with the removal men. I want every typewriter in the building boxed up and brought on the same van – the girls downstairs will have to manage without until we've eliminated their machines as the one the blackmailer used."

The DCS went into the next office. Mrs Wyatt was sitting in one of the armchairs. She looked up, but didn't speak.

"She's not much of a conversationalist, sir," said Locke with faux disappointment.

"No? Well, she has a lot to think about, and the weather isn't likely to rank very high on her list of priorities.

"Take her to the nick, and see her booked in. That's it for you, then – and thanks for your help."

***

Within ten minutes, Haig reported that he had been able to arrange for everything to be removed. "I thought one of the WPCs could supervise the removal at this end, sir, and travel in the van's cab. I'll arrange for someone to supervise the unloading at the other end, so she can walk straight back here afterwards. I doubt she'll be away much above twenty minutes."

"Very sensible. Let's go and see the Wyatts now."

"To me they're coming across as guilty," said Haig as the Yard detectives drove the short distance to West End Central police station. "No protestations of innocence, no demands to see a solicitor. Just silence. Which one do you think is Nemesis?"

"Agreed on the behaviour, Inspector. As for Nemesis, I'd need to talk to them a lot more before plumping for one."

On arrival at the police station in Savile Row, the DCS called for Maria Wyatt to be brought to an interview room first. She was a heavily-built young woman in her late twenties, of average height, with short light-brown hair and rather small features, as though her nose, eyes and mouth, had somehow failed to develop as fully as her head. Both officers found attempts to assess her character quite impossible, as she didn't speak a single word in answer to their questions, and instead sat looking into the distance. She's been primed to be inscrutable, thought the DCS, and managing it pretty well.

"All right Maria," said Bryce eventually. "We're not going to waste any more time on you."

He went to the door, and called for someone to lock the girl up again. "Bring us the mother instead, when you've done that."

A few minutes later Mrs Wyatt was seated at the table.

"Would you like to talk to us, Mrs Wyatt?" enquired Bryce.

"Not really, Chief Superintendent," replied the woman, folding her arms across her chest. "However, since you've dragged me here I'm prepared to listen to you."

"Very well. We have reason to believe that your bureau is a front. Its principal *raison d'être* is to plant servants into households, and then get the less scrupulous ones to report on the peccadilloes of their master or mistress – so that you can blackmail them. You've widened your scope by approaching the staff recruited by the agencies you bought.

"I have no idea how many positive results you get, but even a small proportion must be very profitable. Certainly if some of your recent communications are typical, the price of silence can be extremely expensive."

Mrs Wyatt was unperturbed. "What communications would they be? You have no evidence to suggest that either I, or my daughter, is a blackmailer. Nor will you find any."

"We have statements from some of those who make reports to you, via your direct telephone line."

"Very possibly you do," she laughed. "Listening to tittle-tattle doesn't constitute any offence that I'm aware of, and I challenge you to prove that it does." She stared insolently at the Chief Superintendent, her manner highly provocative. "Go on, Mr Bryce; go right ahead and charge me for listening to gossip, why don't you!"

Mrs Wyatt sat back in her seat, relaxed and evidently immensely pleased with herself. "You arrested me on suspicion of conspiracy to demand money with menaces. So, where's this alleged conspiracy?"

"Between you, your daughter, and a number of domestic servants."

Mrs Wyatt now laughed uproariously. "I don't think so. You'll have a real battle to prove that."

"Well, we'll have to see what we can do – and you'll be kept here overnight while we're doing it. Do you want to see a solicitor?"

"No. I have absolutely no need to waste my money. But when you eventually release us, as you soon must, I shall start a civil action against the Metropolitan Police as well as you, personally, if my business has suffered any harm."

Bryce, impervious to the threats, was nevertheless disappointed with the lack of anything useful from the interview. He felt it was time he played Mrs Wyatt at her own game.

With a confidence that he wasn't actually feeling he smiled back at her and said, "Oh I'm quite sure that we'll find more than enough evidence to charge you. If not at your office, then in your home."

He hoped he sounded convincing, but Wyatt merely narrowed her eyes and sneered.

CHAPTER 20

Bryce and Haig returned to the Yard, and found that Kittow and Drummond had arrived before them.

"The Wyatt's live in a nice enough house, sir, but not huge or especially opulent – more what you'd call comfortable. We didn't need to break in because a daily help opened the door to us.

"We went through the premises systematically, sir, but found absolutely nothing. No lists of names, or files, or anything like that. Just the usual running a home stuff – bills from the butcher, coal merchant, and so on."

"Did you find anything at all to bring away?" asked Haig, perturbed. Having sat through the two Wyatt interviews, he was beginning to share Bryce's feeling that although the women were guilty, the detectives might not find any proof.

"All we've brought back is a typewriter, with some notepaper and envelopes, but it doesn't look like the stationery Nemesis uses."

"Never mind," said Bryce. "We brought back several typewriters from the office ourselves; hopefully one of ours will be the blackmailer's machine if yours isn't."

He turned to Drummond. "When we've finished here, your job will be to take all the typewriters, plus a letter and its envelope, out to Hendon. They can say whether one of the four was used for the correspondence.

"Before you make a start on calling Dorset, Kittow, give Drummond a hand to carry the things to a car."

Bryce signalled Haig to remain. "I have a warrant for Poole's arrest. I'm not sure about the legality of arresting an MP in the precincts of the House, and it's probably better to avoid his ministry too. So, I'm going to try to reach him now, and invite him to come here this afternoon or this evening. We'll interview him together.

"Carry on downstairs for now, and I'll let you know if I can get him."

Haig went back to his own office, and the DCS picked up his telephone. This time, he was more fortunate in locating Poole and was informed that the Minister was in his office, but was presently engaged in a meeting. He would call back shortly.

Bryce had hardly put down the telephone, when his Secretary tapped on the door;

"There's a reporter downstairs, sir; wants to talk about blackmail. The Desk Officer says you left instructions for anyone coming in about that to be put onto you."

"Yes, quite right, Mrs Pickford. Bring him up, please."

A few minutes later, a shambolic-looking individual was shown into the room. Carrying his overcoat on his arm, he was carelessly dressed in a suit that looked as though it hadn't been pressed in a twelvemonth, with a badly-knotted tie that was as shabby as the too-large Homburg on his head. Bryce thought he would have blended in well with the customers hanging around the seedier venues in Soho. None of which altered the fact that Michael Bland was one of the best investigative journalists of the day.

"Hello, Mickey," said Bryce warmly, his hand outstretched. "Sniffing around again?"

"Good afternoon to you as well, Philip," replied the reporter, removing his hat. "You know how it is old boy; crusts need to be earned and wolves must be kept from doors. It's always a case of 'no story, no eat' for me and mine."

Bland spoke with an 'Oxford' accent, but Bryce had never been able to decide whether this was natural, since he had previously heard the man use what seemed like a perfect Birmingham accent, and on a different occasion a Tyneside one. The selection of voices was just one of the journalist's repertoire of ways to blend in with whatever situation he encountered.

"They tell me you've been promoted yet again," said Bland as he took the seat opposite Bryce. "Never happens to me – I'm no nearer the editor's chair than when I first started."

Bryce was impervious to the reporter's hard luck narrative and his down-and-out wardrobe choices. He had once spotted Bland in the best seats at Covent Garden, dressed in immaculate evening wear. "I bet you get paid nearly as much as your editor, though," he said with a grin, "and I shouldn't be surprised if that's a lot more than I make!"

The reporter laughed, and gave an acquiescing nod.

"Anyway, Mickey, I imagine you've received some letters. So have I, as it happens. I doubt if I can help you much just yet, but tell me what you're after."

"Nemesis?" asked the reporter.

Bryce nodded. "Will you let us have your letters to examine?"

"Don't see why not. But I can tell you that we dusted them for prints ourselves. The letters were clean – and the envelopes useless. One posted in Pimlico, the other in South Kensington, if that helps you.

"You'll be aware, Philip, that when we're talking about eminent people there's always potential for a very bad smell, and lots of unwanted associated publicity. Unwanted by the people concerned, that is. But just what we like best. It'd be good for our circulation and my bonus prospects if I could get a scoop on this."

"No doubt it would, Mickey, but you know me – always even-handed. I've never granted an exclusive story to any paper."

"Didn't expect it," laughed the hack, "but I still have to try every time. Anyway, have you identified Nemesis?"

"We're getting close. The investigation is complicated by the fact that we now have to look into the actual allegations."

"Understood, especially as those concern very important people. Do you look on those matters as more important than the original blackmail?"

"I don't rank them in any order. Everything will be looked at; and you can assure your readers that anyone – and I mean absolutely anyone, regardless of status – who has committed an offence will be charged if the evidence warrants it."

"Are you nearing that point yet?"

Bryce hesitated. "I expect to arrest someone later today, in connection with the allegations. Two people are already under arrest regarding the blackmail matter. Presumably you're aware that a man has been charged with the murder of his valet, a matter which is indirectly connected with the blackmail."

"Yes, I am aware, but come on, Philip. I've helped you in the past. I deserve a bit more than what I already know," cajoled the reporter.

"I can't deny you've occasionally been helpful, Mickey, but I balance that against the even more times you've been a real nuisance! Nevertheless, I'll make a suggestion. Hang around the Westminster Magistrates' Court in the morning. I don't promise anything, but I'm anticipating we'll get someone in the dock."

"Suppose I'll have to be content with that," said the reporter. "I'm looking into the valet's background and so on. The information Nemesis has must have come from people like that, mustn't it?"

He looked archly at the DCS, hoping to catch an involuntary reaction to confirm his accurate thrust. Bryce looked back at him blankly and said nothing.

"Oh very well, be an oyster, Philip! I'll get there in the end."

"Not before me, I think," said Bryce, grinning again and shaking hands with the reporter as he rose to leave.

"I hope I'm right about that," he muttered to himself after handing Bland back to his Secretary to escort out.

Unable to concentrate on his reorganisation plans, Bryce sat with his feet on the desk, thinking. He recognised that this bad habit was quite new, and he wondered why it had started. However, he left his feet where they were.

Minutes later, he was jerked out of his reverie by the telephone bell. David Poole was the caller. Bryce asked the MP to visit the Yard. There was a silence.

"Should I bring my solicitor, Chief Superintendent?"

"That's probably a good idea, Minister."

"I see. Well, I've already taken the precaution of talking to him, and we can both be with you at about six o'clock, if that's convenient."

Bryce agreed that it was.

He rang down to Haig, and asked him to come up, at the same time enquiring, "How is Kittow doing?"

"He has one address, and that of the associated parents. It's looking good. Oh, wait a second…he's giving me a thumbs up…he's got the rest."

"Excellent. Bring him up as well."

As soon as the two detectives arrived Bryce gave his orders for the next day. "We want statements, of course. And I want you to telephone me at every stage when you get one signed.

"Now, to keep you in the picture, Kittow. Poole is coming here tonight, and I intend to arrest and probably charge him. I'm letting the Wyatt's sweat for a bit overnight; hopefully we'll get a match with one of the typewriters and be able to proceed against them tomorrow. I intend to invite Hartley in for a chat tomorrow as well.

"Anyway, Kittow, you carry on making arrangements with the Dorset people, and when you've sorted that you should go home."

***

At ten minutes to six, Inspector Haig knocked on Bryce's door.

"Shall I go down and bring Poole and his solicitor up here when they arrive, sir? Or are you going to do this in an interview room?"

"The latter. I certainly don't want a guard of honour for him; I don't want him to feel special at all. I've already told the front desk to stick him and his mouthpiece in the tattiest interview room."

Haig grinned his approval.

"Everything's in place with both the Dorset victims, and one set of parents; we've agreed approximate times. The missing parents are simply out for the evening – their son says he'll get hold of them first thing in the morning. Difficult to tell over the phone, sir, but Kittow got the feeling that all of them are pleased that someone is taking notice after all these years."

"Good. It would be immensely satisfying if they can see some justice, finally. I hope the same will be the case for the girl allegedly defiled by Edward Fletcher, too. I'm not sure that much can be done for those who lost money in Hartley's frauds all those years ago.

"I'll talk to someone in Dorset first thing in the morning, just to say you're in the county for some interviews. Hopefully, we can give them a ready-made case, so they don't even have to do any work.

"You might ask the lads and their parents where the blockage to their complaints originally occurred. I'd like to know if it was the Church, or the police, or both."

The internal telephone rang, and Bryce was told that his visitors had arrived.

"I feel like making them wait for an hour or so, but that would penalise you and me by keeping us away from home that much longer. So let's get it over with."

When the detectives arrived in the interview room they found Poole standing and looking very tense. With him was a small man in late middle age, wearing a neat moustache and an *en brosse* haircut. Bryce couldn't help the irrelevant thought that although the style was once sported by Prussian army officers, this man would never have passed the height requirements. Introductions were effected, and the policemen learned that the solicitor was Bradley Randall, partner in one of the city's most prestigious law firms. Both police officers knew the name, which had appeared in the news reports of a number of notorious cases, but neither had ever met the man.

When everyone was seated, Bryce

proceeded without any preamble. "I have a warrant for your arrest, Minister, on suspicion of conspiracy to pervert the course of justice. Consider yourself under arrest. Please caution Mr Poole, Inspector."

That done, Bryce added, "The warrant also mentions a matter under the Public Bodies Corrupt Practices Act, but that duplicates the first, so I don't propose to waste time on it."

Randall coughed, and adjusted his spectacles. A highly-experienced advocate, he was well-practised in the art of subtly controlling the police interrogations of his clients. "Without making any admissions on behalf of Mr Poole, Chief Superintendent, I wonder whether it might be preferable to consider that secondary legislation first?"

Bryce looked at him coldly. "Preferable for whom, Mr Randall? The maximum penalty following a conviction under the 1889 Act is two years imprisonment. Perverting the course of justice is a Common Law offence, and, if my memory serves, carries a possible sentence of life imprisonment."

"True, but the Act also specifies that my client would be barred from holding public office for seven years, and might lose his pension entitlement in the process."

"With respect, Mr Randall, that cuts no ice whatsoever with me. If Mr Poole is convicted on the Common Law charge, a lot of his other actions will inevitably be aired in the press – regardless as to whether such actions were criminal. I hardly think that the electorate in his constituency would vote for him anyway in the next seven years, whether he was banned from office or not. Indeed, I rather doubt if his party will give much support at all, considering some of the allegations.

"As for your client's Parliamentary pension, I question whether it will form a significant proportion of his retirement income, or that he would even notice its existence if he does succeed in keeping it!"

Randall subsided. Poole didn't lift his eyes from the table in front of him.

Bryce spoke again. "It comes down to this, Mr Randall. Does your client want to make a statement? You can have a bit more time, if you need it."

"Thank you, no. I have already advised my client to say nothing further at this stage, and I stand by that advice."

"As you wish." The DCS switched his gaze to the Minister. "David Poole, I charge you that, between December the 4th and December 6th, 1947, you conspired with Leslie Fletcher to pervert the course of justice.

"You will be held here overnight, Minister, and will appear before a magistrate at Westminster tomorrow."

Poole seemed to age and shrink in stature

as he listened. He spoke for the first time. "I'm not a minister any longer, Chief Superintendent. I submitted a letter of resignation to the PM just before coming here. I have also taken steps to apply for the Chiltern Hundreds. I imagine that appointment is more-or-less immediate, so I won't even be an MP for many more hours.

"Thank you, by the way, for not piling on the humiliation by arresting me elsewhere.

"Can you say what's happening about the blackmailer?"

"We're pursuing the matter very actively. And, in case you think otherwise, when we find the culprit we will certainly prosecute him or her. Go with Inspector Haig, now. He'll get you 'booked in for the night', as we euphemistically put it."

Bryce and Randall were left standing in the interview room.

"Presumably you'll represent him tomorrow?" enquired the DCS. "You have at least a chance of getting bail – we won't oppose an application."

"Yes, thank you. I'll certainly try. And then we'll find counsel for the Assizes, presumably in Sussex. But all that will be needed is mitigation. Poole will plead guilty. What a mess."

"We have the letters he received, but has he shown you transcripts?"

"No, but he's been open about the other things he's been accused of doing. You mentioned them earlier, of course. Not offences, in my view, and I don't see how the Crown can allude to them in the criminal case."

Randall offered his hand. "I know your background, Chief Superintendent. Just think. In other circumstances I might be offering you a brief for the defence of Mr Poole!"

Bryce smiled as he shook hands, and was quick with his riposte. "Not necessarily. I might have already been lined up for the prosecution!"

With Randall gone, the DCS joined Haig, who was still talking to the Custody Sergeant.

"Result, sir," said the Inspector.

"Yes; and Randall has just told me that Poole will plead guilty when the matter comes to trial."

"The Chiltern Hundreds, sir – I've heard of them, but never really understood the function. What are they?"

"Nothing more than the remnant of a tradition. A member of parliament isn't permitted to resign. That dates back to the early eighteenth century, when the Commons passed a resolution to that effect. Fifty or so years later, the Commons also decided that a member couldn't be independent if he accepted an 'office of profit' from the Crown without the consent of Parliament. So a member appointed to such an 'office' is disqualified from sitting. There used to be several such 'offices' kept on the shelf in readiness, as it were, but I believe only two remain in use. Crown Steward and Bailiff of either the Chiltern Hundreds, or the Manor of Northstead.

"It's a bit of a legal farce really – apparently neither appointment actually carries a salary!"

CHAPTER 21

Wednesday 8th November, 1950

Bryce drove into Westminster with no very clear idea as to how the day should be organised. As he drove, he continued to plan.

Haig and Kittow would be safely off to Dorset, so that much was fixed. For his part, he would have to make a decision very soon about the two Wyatt women currently held in West End Central. He would either have to charge them – and he couldn't think what charge would possibly stick – or release them.

Then there was Poole. Having told Randall that the police wouldn't oppose an application for bail, he would have to speak to whoever was prosecuting at Westminster court, and instruct him accordingly.

Next to be considered was Lord Hartley. Bryce resolved to invite him in 'for a talk'. As the end result was probably going to be unsatisfactory from the police point of view, he was not looking forward to that.

Finally, there was the Bishop. Bryce

mentally turned over the idea of pre-empting the findings that Haig seemed likely to produce, and call the Bishop in. He rejected this, and told himself to be patient.

He parked his car and went upstairs to his office. Mrs Pickford, who was a conscientious timekeeper, had arrived before him as usual. She handed him a note as he passed through her office, telling him that this was the only message.

The three short lines informed him that the laboratory at Hendon had called. None of the four typewriters supplied was used in typing either the letter or the envelope. There was no possibility of error.

Although Bryce had hoped for better, this news wasn't entirely unexpected. It had occurred to him yesterday that Mrs Wyatt's certainty that there would be no evidence against her wasn't founded on thin air. Her manner, both at the bureau and in the police station, had been extremely confident.

He thanked his Secretary for the note and said, "See if you can get hold of Lord Hartley for me, Mrs Pickford. Invite him to come and see me as soon as possible – today if it's convenient. His private number is in the papers on my desk. I'm off to court."

The Magistrates' Court was only a few hundred yards away, and as he walked his mind went back to the various blackmail letters.

How had all the information reached the

author? He was satisfied that this question was now correctly answered – disloyal servants had obtained it, and passed it to the Wyatts. But it followed that if neither of them was Nemesis, then they must have passed the information to someone else.

Suddenly, Bryce had a new thought. He stood stock still to process it, and immediately had to apologise to the pedestrian who ran into him from behind.

Moving aside to stand against a wall, the solution suddenly flashed into his mind. He actually spoke out loud, "How can I have been so stupid?" worrying a pair of ladies trying to walk around him.

After a quick apology, he resumed his journey, still thinking. At the courthouse, he found the prosecutor in the remand court, and briefed him on the Poole matter. The final decision on bail would be for the Magistrate, but Bryce instructed the prosecuting police officer not to oppose an application from Mr Randall.

He waved across the courtroom foyer to Mickey Bland, but didn't speak.

Not feeling like a long walk up to West End Central police station, he hailed a taxi to Savile Row. At the police station, he instructed the driver to wait. Inside, he was greeted by the Desk Sergeant, who knew him quite well.

"You're holding the two Wyatt women for me, Sergeant. Can you get someone to bring them to me in an interview room, one at a time. Won't take but a minute each, and then he can take them back again."

The daughter was brought first.

"I won't beat about the bush," said Bryce. "I charge you with conspiracy to demand money with menaces. You'll be brought before a court tomorrow. If you want a solicitor, mention it to the Custody Sergeant as you go past."

Miss Wyatt looked as if she might actually speak, but didn't. She was taken away, and a few minutes later her mother was produced.

Bryce repeated his earlier words exactly, varying only in the matter of Christian name, and to mention that he had also charged Maria.

"I really didn't think you would charge us, Chief Superintendent. On your head be it. I'll get a solicitor to represent both of us – there isn't going to be a 'cut-throat defence'. Oh yes, I am familiar with the argot."

"I'm so pleased, Mrs Wyatt. I hope you're also familiar with the term 'imprisonment for life'. Although I rather think your actual sentence will be between ten and twelve years. You won't find life in Holloway a bed of roses."

"You can dream, Chief Superintendent, and you can threaten, but you'll never convict either of us!"

When Mrs Wyatt, still smiling, had been taken away, Bryce went to talk to the Sergeant again. He explained the charges he had just laid.

"Hold them until tomorrow morning. Then get them to Westminster Magistrates' court. I'll sort out the prosecution."

Outside, he climbed into his waiting taxi, barely fifteen minutes since he had left it, and told the driver to take him to Scotland Yard.

Back in his office, he carefully read through the interview material the detectives had so far collated between them, and contemplated how to adduce the proof he would need to back up his new theory. In the absence of his two more experienced officers, he called down and told Drummond to come up.

When the young detective arrived Bryce showed him the Hendon Lab note.

"So this means we've got nothing at all on the Wyatts sir?"

"'Fraid so. I do have a theory, though. Go along to Somerset House. I have no idea how the system works there – or even if they have a system. It may not be possible, in a reasonable time, to find what I want – but do your best anyway."

Bryce gave Drummond some detailed instructions, and sent the young man on his way.

He picked up the telephone, and made a call to Cambridge. After some difficulty, he reached the person he wanted. Identifying himself, he suggested the man should call him back immediately on the famous WHItehall 1212 number to reassure himself that his caller was a genuine police officer. The man did so, and Bryce asked him for some information.

"Odd thing to ask," said the voice. "Never had a question like that before. It'll take me half an hour at least to establish. I'll call you back."

In fact, it was nearly an hour before the call was returned. But the information provided brought a broad smile of triumph to the DCS's face. He asked a supplementary question which was answered immediately, and he gave warm thanks to his helper.

***

Bryce spent the next hour drafting his report on the case – or rather cases – so far. He was about to go for some lunch when the external telephone rang.

The caller was Haig, reporting that he and Kittow had interviewed both Frank Porterfield and his parents, and had obtained statements from all three.

"Crystal clear, sir, and very nasty. Porterfield was a boy of eleven at the time. Charrington was the vicar of the village, and one day after Matins, he invited the boy to come across to the vicarage.

"The boy went home in tears – and incidentally, it's possible that a maid in the vicarage knew what happened, and stored that information for years, until the chance came to pass it on to the Wyatts. We can look into that."

"Anyway, the boy got home, and told his mother. She went to the village policeman, and got nowhere. He said that her boy was a spiteful liar, and that a good thrashing would sort him out. The bobby refused to take the matter seriously.

"The father went round to the vicarage, probably doffing his cap to the abuser, but Charrington said the same thing – the boy was making things up.

"These aren't educated people, sir. The parents simply didn't know what else to do.

"They withdrew the boy from the choir, of course, but the father worked for the local squire, and the family lived in a tied cottage. The parents didn't dare to make any more fuss. They didn't even take the boy to a doctor.

"I mentioned the other similar case, and it was news to all the Porterfields. They wished they'd known at the time that there was another family in the same boat – there would have been strength in numbers.

"These statements are enough to proceed against the Bishop, if you want to make a move, sir. We're seeing the Rhodes family – the son and parents together – at one o'clock."

"Well done, Inspector. Call again when you've seen them, and then come straight back."

Bryce paid a quick visit to the staff canteen, then returned to his desk to see if he could contact the Bishop. Speaking to the same unctuous aide as before, he was informed that the Prelate was attending the House of Lords, and was not expected back in the palace until the following day.

Thinking it almost certain that Charrington would be staying at the Goring again, Bryce called the hotel. He learned that the Bishop was indeed staying, but was currently elsewhere. However, the helpful receptionist added that his lordship had indicated he would be dining on the premises.

Well satisfied, the DCS settled down to his report writing.

At two o'clock, Haig called again. "Exactly the same story, sir. The boys knew each other, of course, although being a couple of years apart in age they weren't close friends. Neither had any idea that the other had also been assaulted. Same thing about the second complaint, except that in the year between the incidents a new village bobby had been appointed. He was just as disbelieving as the first.

"Cast-iron statements again, sir. Oh, and we have the names of some of the vicar's servants at the time – everyone knew everyone in the village, of course. The Rhodes family have no idea where they are now, but if we could trace them, and link them with one of the agencies, it might help with both parts of this case."

"Yes, we'll certainly look into that. What time do you think you'll get back?"

"Given a fair wind, I suppose about six, sir."

"Good – I'll be here. You and I have another task tonight."

***

Bryce had no time to concentrate on his plans, because almost immediately he received a summons to visit the Assistant Commissioner. As he made his way through the building, he wondered if another well-connected personage had been in contact to complain about a blackmail letter.

The AC greeted him as he walked in. "I won't take up much of your time, Philip. This package arrived yesterday, addressed to the Commissioner. As Sir Harold was away, and the label said 'personal and confidential', it wasn't opened until he came in a few minutes ago. Basically it's an affidavit made by Julian Barratt. He states that he conspired with Lord Hartley to defraud various people, so obviously this is connected with your case. There are a lot of other papers giving more details. You've been looking into this chap, presumably?"

Bryce nodded. "We have some very useful testimony from one of his servants."

"Right – well you can add these to your collection. Are you making other progress?"

"Yes, sir. I have two women in custody – they run an employment bureau, which we believe is the centre of the information-gathering ring. They'll appear in court tomorrow charged with conspiracy to commit blackmail.

"I've arrested David Poole, and charged him with conspiracy to pervert the course of justice. He'll plead guilty to that, apparently. And he's already resigned both his ministerial office and his seat. He was due before the beak today. I haven't heard the outcome, but I said we wouldn't oppose an application for bail.

"Tonight, I'm arresting the Bishop of Crewe – he'll be charged with serious offences against children."

The AC was staring at Bryce in astonishment.

"Good God, man! I wasn't really expecting the complainants to be arrested ahead of the blackmailer. What about the letter writer? One of the women, was it?"

"I don't think so, sir. They – mother and daughter – acted as the conduit. I believe they passed the information on to Nemesis. Quite possible that the mother is the prime mover, though. She's intelligent and educated, but I believe there's a third wheel.

"Anyway, I'm seeking another warrant in the morning, and we'll see what we can find."

"Well, if all this sticks, Philip, you've done a remarkable job."

Bryce, quietly pleased with the praise, said, "While I'm in your good books, sir, I'd just like to ask your authority to make a few initial changes.

I'll give you much more detail in due course, but I'd like to make three promotions immediately. They can easily be paid for by the officers I'll be wanting to get rid of."

"Go on," said the AC.

"I'd like to push Jack Nunn up to DCI and have him as my administrative manager. I'd also like to make DC Kittow up to sergeant. Finally, I'd like to bring in a DC from another force, and promote him to sergeant too. I've worked with him, and he's a really good man. He may not accept, of course."

"Do it," replied the AC. "I'll give you written authority within half an hour."

"I appreciate that, sir," said Bryce, who had been expecting to have to work a great deal harder to get what he wanted.

He returned to his office, and started to attack his seemingly self-replenishing mound of paperwork while he waited for his team.

CHAPTER 22

Mrs Pickford was covering her typewriter prior to going home when DC Drummond diffidently put his head into the room and asked if he could see the Chief Superintendent. Knowing he was involved in the present case, the Secretary waved him to Bryce's door.

"Bit of a job, sir, but after a few hours I got lucky – here's what you asked for." He handed over a document with a happy smile. "I don't know how you worked it out, though!"

Bryce looked at the paper, and then grinned at the young detective.

"Well done, Drummond! This will be very valuable. Not a hundred percent proved yet, but I'm confident we're getting there.

"As to how I worked it out – I'll explain that when we're all back together again. Incidentally, we now have cast-iron statements from the parties in Dorset.

As he spoke, there was a knock on the door. Haig and Kittow came in, both looking tired but happy. Kittow placed the statements on the desk.

"Take seats, gentlemen," said Bryce. "All of you have done well today, and I'm ready to tell you what I've been up to."

The DCS gave a brief report on his charging the two women, and Barratt's affidavit. He paused. "I believe we finally know the identity of Nemesis."

The faces of Haig and Kittow registered astonishment.

"Drummond already knows because I sent him to do some fresh digging today, and as a result of what he found he's realised the probable solution. But he still wants to know how I worked it out.

"I thought about the various letters, particularly the two sent to the police. In the first, as Mr Haig queried, how did the writer know that anyone had gone to the police?

"I discussed that with you all and I came around to the popular view: the blackmailer either guessed, or knew all the victims well enough to have assumed which of them would contact the police.

"But I realised that if the Coates agency connection was correct, it was far more likely that Nemesis *didn't* know the Westminster trio – or any of the victims – because all Nemesis would ever receive were the reports from the servants via the Wyatts. At that point I accepted it must be guesswork.

"Then our second letter came. There was a

line in that which we all read – but we all failed to spot its significance. The writer said he was sorry Barratt was dead. But Barratt had dismissed his servants before killing himself. And there had been no report in the newspapers.

"So – how could the writer have known that Barratt was dead?"

Kittow responded almost immediately, with a look of consternation on his face. "One of us told him?"

Bryce gave a sigh and a nod.

"Nemesis is Barratt's solicitor, then?" asked Kittow. He was particularly remembering how much he had revealed to the lawyer about the recipients of the blackmail letters who had already contacted the police. "He's a very educated man and words are his livelihood, I'll bet he could write those letters, no bother." He gave his forehead a light slap with the palm of his hand. "And I was there specifically to tell him that Barratt was dead, into the bargain!"

Bryce shook his head. "No, Kittow, it wasn't Gibbs. Drummond, whilst doing his records trawl, has completely eliminated Gibbs as a suspect; you gave away nothing that you shouldn't have done."

"It's Marlowe, then?" asked Haig.

This time Bryce nodded. "Yes, I believe so; and I was the one who told him." He looked at Kittow, and gave his own forehead a mock slap.

"This morning, I tried to establish links

between him and the Coates set up. We have one that I'm extremely happy with, and one that's more circumstantial. Later today I hope to find a third link – probably even more circumstantial, but every scrap of evidence helps us over the 'burden of proof' hurdle."

"What made you think of Marlowe, sir?" asked Kittow.

"It crossed my mind that blackmailers are often solitary practitioners, but with the Wyatt women we already had two people involved. Having raided their office and their home and found nothing, the conclusion could only be that there was a third location which was the repository holding all the incriminating information – the dirt on the employers; who the Wyatt's paid and how much; and the typewriter.

"The more I thought about the size of the Nemesis operation – bigger and more wide-ranging than anything else I've ever heard of – the more I found myself thinking about the potential risk to the Wyatt's of working with someone with whom they didn't have an extremely close and trusting connection. That was when I decided Nemesis was most likely to be another Wyatt of some description, either by marriage, or by birth.

"I despatched Drummond to Somerset House and told him to start pulling out the records for every woman called Beatrice Wyatt, of which, he tells me, there are a surprising number! From those records he had to note the women's former names – whether maiden or previously married.

"Turns out our Mrs Wyatt had been married before."

"To a Mr Marlowe?"

Bryce nodded. "I'm satisfied that Dr Marlowe is Wyatt's son by her first marriage.

"While Drummond was in Somerset House, I was telephoning Houghton College in Cambridge. Marlowe himself told us he had been an undergraduate there, and it didn't take long for the bursar to dig out the file with his original registration. His next of kin was recorded as his mother, Beatrice Wyatt. Maria is presumably his half-sister. We'll round up all the associated certificates to prove the family relationships later.

"The second circumstantial indicator that Nemesis was Marlowe was a much weaker clue. Of the first six recipients we know of, the allegations in five of the first letters were quickly proved to have substance. Not necessarily criminal substance, of course, but the point is that in not one of those five cases were the allegations groundless. The allegations in Marlowe's letter, however, were completely untrue."

"That seems like a pretty good clue to me, sir, now you've spelled it out," said Drummond, sounding unsure, "what am I missing?"

"The fact that Nemesis told us there were ten letters, and we have no reason to believe that was a lie, since we know that Higgins received a letter. That made a total of seven letters we knew about. But that still left three more letters we didn't see, so for all we knew those three also had baseless allegations."

He fell silent. To his astonishment, his little team, already grinning while he was talking, spontaneously began to clap.

"Pack it in," Bryce growled. "I – and indeed all of you – should have picked up the point about Barratt's death far sooner. Still, hopefully we're really closing in on Nemesis now."

"But why would Marlowe send himself a letter, sir?" asked Kittow. "If he hadn't done that we'd probably never have known he existed."

"That's right," agreed the DCS, "and maybe it was a case of being arrogantly over-confident – a trait I could well believe he's inherited from his mother, given what I've seen of that lady so far. But I think he did it in order to have a good chance of learning about our progress, and lines of investigation. And of course he even suggested – very plausibly – how his letter might have reached him by mistake.

"There are lots of loose ends to be tied up. We can try to get telephone records for calls from Coates – see if we can prove calls to Marlowe. We also need to check with the WPCs on site about any calls they've received.

"But the main event tomorrow will be the four of us raiding Marlowe's house, following which we can trace and interview more staff like Aggie who were involved, and get their statements. First thing in the morning, Inspector, go and find a magistrate and fix up the paperwork for that."

Haig nodded. "How great is the risk do you think, sir, that Marlowe will try to contact his mother, and that when he finds he can't do so he might destroy evidence?"

"There's undoubtedly a risk, yes. But even if he guesses that she and his half-sister have been arrested, he'll know they won't mention him, and he'll bank on the fact that without their co-operation we'll never make the link with him. So hopefully he'll have done nothing.

"As for tonight," he looked at Haig and Kittow, "you've had a long journey, so you two get off home. Drummond and I will arrest the Bishop. We'll have to leave Hartley for another day."

***

Bryce and Drummond drove round to Mayfair in Bryce's Triumph Roadster, a separate, marked police Wolseley accompanying them. This arrangement was necessary because the Chief Superintendent wanted to go on to Arnos Grove and then straight home afterwards, rather than trekking back to the Yard. He could then leave

Drummond and the uniformed officer to take the Bishop to the police station in a police vehicle.

Bryce parked near the hotel. The receptionist gave them a friendly welcome, recognising the Chief Superintendent as a previous visitor of the Bishop's. He was alarmed when the Chief Superintendent this time showed him a warrant card, but asked no questions as he confirmed the room number.

Bryce and Drummond took the stairs and knocked on the Bishop's door. The Prelate opened it, visibly blenching at the sight of the detectives.

The DCS came straight to the point. "Caspar Charrington, you are under arrest on suspicion of serious crimes under the Offences Against The Person Act. You do not have to say anything, but anything you do say may be taken down and used in evidence. Get your hat and coat."

The Bishop said nothing, but looked as if he would burst into tears at any moment.

The detectives marched their charge past the hotel receptionist again, Bryce giving the man a polite nod of thanks before handing the Bishop over to the waiting policeman outside for the ride to West End Central police station with Drummond.

"Blimey, sir! You trying to fill all our cells single-handed?" exclaimed the Custody Sergeant, letting out a long whistle when he realised the rank of his newest detainee. "We've never had a bishop in here before!"

"I hope to have one more client for you tomorrow, Sergeant," said Bryce. "But you'll have got the Wyatt women off to court by then."

Charrington stood silently and miserably while he was booked in.

With the formalities finalised, Bryce addressed the Bishop. "I don't feel like interviewing you tonight. I'll come along and talk to you some time tomorrow. If you want a solicitor, the Sergeant here will arrange it – or you can make a call yourself if you wish.

As Charrington was led away, the DCS addressed the Duty Officer again. "Sergeant, have your people keep a close eye on him. We've already had one suicide in this case, and I don't want another escaping the consequences of his actions."

Outside, Bryce asked Drummond where he lived.

"Neasden, sir. I'll just walk to Piccadilly Circus and get the tube."

"I'll see you in the morning then. Good night."

The DCS drove on to Arnos Grove. It was getting late, but he wanted to either confirm or eliminate his latest hunch that evening. When speaking to the Houghton College Bursar in Cambridge, to establish Marlowe's next of kin, Bryce had made an apparently irrelevant and unrelated enquiry. Armed with the information received, the DCS had asked his secretary to check when Basil Eccles would be on duty again, as there was a supplementary question he wanted to put to the London Transport man. Learning that he would be working a late shift that day, he had decided to visit him.

He found a convenient parking place and walked through the main hallway of the station, past the passimeter, and down onto the Eastbound platform. The guard was just waving off a train. As soon as this operation was completed, the Chief Superintendent approached him and introduced himself.

"You gave one of my men some helpful information the other day," said Bryce, "but I'm wondering if you might not have a bit more."

"How'd you reckon that then?" asked Eccles cheerfully.

Bryce produced the notes from Drummond's pocketbook. "You described our suspect's coat, hat, and briefcase as being either 'dark' or 'black'. But you didn't describe his scarf – you just said he was wearing one."

Eccles looked back at Bryce closely, frowned, and then inclined his head, first to the right and then to the left, his eyes darting upwards as he searched his memory before settling on the DCS again. He slowly smiled. "Well blow me down! Yer wearin' a similar sort of scarf yerself – same dark green colour, I reckon – but I recall now his had a mustard yellow stripe where I see yours has blue."

The DCS was now treated to a display of Eccles' sucking air through his remaining teeth while the man considered why he hadn't described the scarf to Drummond.

"I knew 'e was wearin' a scarf, 'n' o' course that's what I told your constable. But you don't think to describe a man's scarf like you would a 'at or coat, or 'is height and age. Different for ladies' scarves p'raps – bright colours 'n matchin' bits 'n pieces. But I'll definitely swear now to the scarf 'e was wearin'."

Bryce was very happy with this thoughtful response, and the description he had just been given of the scarf – the colours being as described by the Houghton College Bursar. Since the London Transport man was a possible witness, the DCS could hardly give him a tip before he gave evidence. However, Bryce thanked the station employee warmly.

He drove home, feeling well satisfied with the way the investigation was going.

Tiredness overtook him as soon as he put his key into the front door lock. After kissing his wife he collapsed into an armchair.

"I suggest we have our meal on trays tonight," said Veronica.

"Bless you, Vee, I'm just not feeling like sitting at the table."

His meal was soon brought to him, and he gave his wife a précis of his day's work.

"I hate the idea of how blackmailers operate – the fear they can generate in their victims – but I can't help feeling that this one was doing things which exposed some real wickedness," said Veronica. "Will he be treated more leniently?"

"Not at all. Don't forget that that as a direct result of his activities, one man committed murder, and another suicide. I'm sure that he caused a lot of unknown misery to others as well. I expect to find that a lot of money has been successfully extracted from lesser marks than the ones we know about."

Anticipating another busy day, Bryce retired to bed an hour before his usual time.

CHAPTER 23

Thursday 9th November 1950

In the office the next morning, Mrs Pickford reported that she had been unable to contact Lord Hartley the previous day, even though she had been trying until well after six o'clock. Bryce called Hartley's private number himself. To his surprise, the peer himself answered immediately, and the DCS invited him to come into Scotland Yard for a chat. There was a short silence at the other end of the line.

"Are you arresting me, Bryce? As I said the other day, the original allegations don't suggest anything illegal. Now the Nemesis swine has made further allegations. I deny those, and I warn you that you can never prove anything."

"You are being invited to come in as a free man, m'lord. But depending on how our discussion goes, I don't say that you will leave as one. However, if you choose not to come, then I shall certainly send men to arrest you."

"Very well," snarled Hartley, evidently hugely annoyed, "I'll bring my solicitor. Will this afternoon suit you?"

An appointment was agreed for three o'clock, and the call was terminated.

For the second day running, Bryce walked down to the Westminster Magistrates' Court. It was drizzling, and he needed his umbrella.

At the court, he spoke to the same prosecuting inspector he had seen the previous day, and briefed him on the case against the Wyatt women. This time he instructed the prosecutor to oppose bail.

He didn't hang around to see the case called on, but returned to his office. Haig was waiting for him, and confirmed that a warrant had been granted to search Marlowe's home.

Kittow and Drummond were summoned upstairs.

"Right, there's no point in hanging about," said the DCS. "We'll take two cars. I can't see Marlowe running away, but you go round to the back all the same, Kittow, just in case. Come with me in my car and I'll take you into the service alley that runs behind the terrace, before I join Haig and Drummond at the front. Wait at the back door, and we'll let you in – if it's open just come straight in, of course.

"Let's go."

As the Chief Superintendent had anticipated, there was no trouble. Once again Marlowe answered the door himself. He seemed momentarily taken aback to see three officers, before recovering his poise.

"Do come in, gentlemen. We'll go into the sitting room, if you don't mind."

"We'll actually be taking a look at all your rooms, Dr Marlowe," said Bryce, "and we'll be doing that whether you mind or not. I have a warrant to search these premises. You, incidentally, are under arrest on suspicion of blackmail. Drummond, find the back door and let Kittow in.

"Caution him, please, Inspector."

Marlowe said nothing in response to the caution.

Drummond returned with Kittow and was immediately instructed to handcuff the academic and take him into another room. "I don't want him trying to destroy evidence while we look around.

"Inspector, you and I will make a start in the study. Kittow, you check in every other room, upstairs and down. See what you can find."

The study was quickly established to be the nerve centre of the Nemesis blackmail enterprise. Large wooden cabinets held numerous suspension files. Bryce flicked through some of these and immediately realised they stored the crucial evidence the detectives were seeking. The label on each file bore the name of the victim, and on the first sheet of paper was the name and position of what appeared to be Nemesis's spy in the household.

Subsequent sheets were treasury tagged together in a systematic way. The first detailed the date and the information the Wyatts were given. The next was a carbon copy of the blackmail letter, which included the *'contribution'* to be made and how it should be paid. The following sheet recorded the amount Nemesis had authorised should be paid to the informant. Many of the files were thick with these tagged sheets, and Bryce was sickened to see how regularly some victims had been fleeced.

One of the thinner files was labelled 'Arnold Smithers'. Bryce read the entire history of that gentleman's liaison with a girl from one of the Tiller dancing troupes. Mr Smithers was a relatively new victim, hence his slimmer file. He had paid a total of one hundred and eighty pounds to Nemesis in the last year alone, attempting to stave off the threat that his wife *'...so generous to you, Mr Smithers, considering your personal penury...'* would undoubtedly withdraw not only her largesse, but also herself from their marriage, were she ever to find out *'...how well – and indeed how often – you have enjoyed the nubile Miss Norma Reed'*.

Riffling through drawers until he came to a file marked 'Galbraith', Bryce was not surprised to see that it was indeed the valet Crossland who had betrayed his employer.

Having seen enough to confirm all his suspicions, he called across to Haig, who was delving into the deep bottom drawer of a large desk. "Plenty here for a conviction. What else have you found, Inspector?"

"A typewriter and a supply of paper which looks mighty like the stuff Nemesis uses." The DI held aloft a ledger. "And this book is their accounts, sir; a running total of blackmail income from victims, and outgoings to informants."

"Good," said Bryce, assessing the quantity of assembled material to be removed. "Unless Kittow finds anything else we should be able to pile what we need into one of the cars, and put Marlowe in the other."

Almost as he spoke, Kittow came into the study. "Nothing anywhere, sir; sorry."

"No matter. I believe we have all we'll need in here. "Let's join Drummond."

The three officers found their colleague in the dining room, where he and Marlowe were sitting in silence.

"Has he said anything, Constable?" asked Bryce.

"Not a peep out of him, sir."

"Okay. Inspector, you and Drummond take him out, lock him in my car and wait with him for a minute while I give Kittow some instructions.

With Marlowe removed, Bryce spoke again.

"I'm leaving you and Drummond to bring

everything in here back to the yard. Dump all the blackmail files and the accounts book – not the typewriter and paper – in my room at the Yard.

"Then, I want you to sit at my table and list the names on each file, together with the name and position within whichever households the informant has been working.

"After that, make another list, this time using the accounts book. Include against each name all the sums of money going in or out – you'll see what I mean.

"What I need are two simple transcripts of the basic information in both places. Got that?"

Kittow nodded, happy again that he was being given tasks which not long ago would have been Inspector Haig's responsibility as a sergeant.

Bryce hadn't finished delegating. "When Drummond comes back, you can give him two jobs. First, get him to take Marlowe's typewriter and some of the paper to the lab. Same request as before. He can collect the other machines while he's there, and return them to Lower Regent Street. I can't think what use they'll be to Coates now, but we don't want them clogging up the Yard.

"I really don't know what to suggest he tells the two clerks. I'm sorry for them, but there's nothing we can do. I don't think we need bother about their statements after all, but Drummond should ensure he has their addresses. Then he'll have to evict them. Kibble can lock the place up. The WPCs should make their reports to me as soon as possible. Got all that?"

Kittow looked up from his pocketbook. "Yes, sir."

Bryce left the study. Instead of turning towards the front door, he went further down the hallway to the crammed hallstand. He removed a scarf, a trilby, and a charcoal overcoat from a hook. The scarf was exactly as Eccles had described – dark green with thin yellow stripes. He doubted he would need the clothing now, but it could be used as additional rather than crucial evidence. Had the raid been unsuccessful (Marlowe perhaps making daily contact with his mother and sister and realising something had gone badly wrong when he couldn't reach them), the scarf and Basil Eccles' subsequent identification might have proved critical. In any event, the Chief Superintendent always aimed to secure as much evidence as possible, and hooked the garments over his arm.

At the car, Bryce told Drummond to return to the house and follow Kittow's instructions.

To Marlowe he said, "We're taking you to West End Central police station. You can talk to us there, if you wish. You may, of course, have a solicitor. You drive, Inspector."

The palaeontologist maintained his silence. At the police station he was booked in, the Custody Officer raising his eyebrows at the DCS but saying nothing.

"Get him into an interview room, Inspector, and we'll have what may be a very one-sided conversation if he adopts the same attitude as the Wyatt women did."

The three men sat down in the same room in which the mother and daughter had been interviewed.

"I need hardly say that we have enough evidence to convict you ten times over, Nemesis. I'm not sure how frequently you speak to Coates, so you may not yet be aware that your mother and half-sister are already in custody."

Marlowe appeared very calm. He gave an exaggerated sigh.

"Well, Chief Superintendent, an excellent and very profitable activity comes to an end. I know Maria and my mother would never grass on me, so I assume I made a mistake?"

"You did. As Nemesis, you shouldn't have known that Barratt was dead. His servants – including Aggie Saunders, your informant – had been discharged and had left the house hours before he shot himself. In fact, I hadn't even given you his name; I just referred to him as 'a recipient in Kent'."

"Oh dear; quite the blunder, then. But surely you accept that as far as the three big fish were concerned, I was doing my civic duty? Laying information before the police."

"In a sense, yes. But the proper way to expose these people would have been to provide whatever evidence you obtained directly to the police. I accept it would have had to be done anonymously, to avoid having to explain how you came by it.

"No. You're a professional blackmailer, Dr Marlowe, and the most superficial glance in your files shows you've been engaged in this filthy business on a smaller scale for years. Then, suddenly, more – and potentially far more profitable – dirt reached you. Initially at least, you saw the possibility of big rewards from important people.

"The irony for me is that if, from the outset, you'd told each of the three Westminster men everything you had on them, the chances are they'd have paid up and never contacted the Commissioner.

"Anyway, as a result of your activities one man has killed himself, and another has been driven to murder. It may be that, when we meticulously analyse your admirably comprehensive records, we'll find that there have been other tragic consequences to lay at your door.

"While I have no sympathy with people like Poole and Charrington, I have no sympathy with you either. The law provides for blackmailers to get life imprisonment. The judge will probably hand down a term of fifteen years to whichever of you was the moving force behind all this – and I'm guessing that was your mother. If so, you're probably looking at ten or twelve years yourself. A pity hard labour has just been abolished."

Bryce looked dispassionately at his prisoner. "Do you want to make a statement?"

"Has my mother brought in a solicitor?"

"I believe so, yes."

"Then I should like to consult the same man, before deciding how to play this."

The glibness of this last comment irked the DCS immensely. Remembering a sentence in the first letter Nemesis had addressed to the police, Bryce delivered a biting put-down. "I do hope how you decide to 'play this' will afford you some amusement. After all, as you told me in one of your letters, what is life if one cannot enjoy a laugh?

"In the meantime, Simon Marlowe, I charge you with conspiring with Beatrice Wyatt and Maria Wyatt to demand money with menaces from various persons on various occasions, contrary to Section 29 of the Larceny Act.

"That's a holding charge. We may add more specific charges later. In any case, we can tidy that one up when finalising the indictment, putting in the dates, names of the victims, etc. Your solicitor can discuss that with me in a day or so."

Bryce stood and opened the door to the interview room, telling the local constable who had sat in on the interview, "Take him back to the Custody Sergeant, please, and get him locked up."

Bryce and Haig chatted for a few minutes to allow the booking-in process to take place. Returning to the desk, the Chief Superintendent spoke to the Sergeant again.

"Marlowe is Mrs Wyatt's son. Ship him down to see the Westminster beak tomorrow morning. See if you can find the same solicitor she had. I don't know if he'll want to come here today, or wait until his client arrives for the remand hearing tomorrow.

"For now, please bring out the Bishop. We don't want to speak to him, but unfortunately it has to be done."

The interview with the Bishop was short. He had not requested a solicitor, and looked to be in a pitiful state.

"Remember you are still under caution, Bishop. Do you want to say anything?"

The Prelate shook his head.

"Very well. You are charged with two counts of sexual assault, contrary to the Offences Against The Person Act. We'll add the names and dates later. You know what those offences are. Given that we're talking about child victims, and the fact that you were in a position of authority, you're looking at twenty years inside.

"Yours is an interesting situation. There

doesn't seem to be a standard procedure for unfrocking a priest in the Church of England, but I'm sure the authorities will feel they must do something. Much easier in the Catholic Church, although I don't know how the Pope would deal with a bishop nowadays. It's nearly four hundred years since Cranmer was unfrocked.

"However, I've looked up the relevant law for your situation, Bishop. It seems that under the Clergy Discipline Act any or all your matters could be tried in a Church court – for someone of your rank probably the Chancery Court of York rather than an ordinary Consistory court.

"But that is unlikely, because the ordinary criminal courts will get hold of you first. Conveniently, the Act also covers any clergyman who is convicted in a secular court and sentenced to a term of imprisonment. In such a case, the bishop must deprive the offender of his living, and has the option of deposing him from holy orders. I assume in your case the Archbishop will deprive you of your bishopric. Given that the Act goes on a good deal about immoral behaviour, I can't believe that he won't defrock you as well.

"The police won't proceed with the allegations of simony, or of selling Church plate; those matters will be passed to the Church authorities, to be dealt with as they think fit. But under the circumstances, I doubt if the Archbishop will bother to proceed either. He'll have quite enough to act on without those.

"You need a solicitor. Do you have one in mind, or do you want us to find one? Failing that, the magistrate might offer you the chance of trying for a dock brief in the morning, but that's a bit hit or miss, even if there happen to be any counsel in court."

Charrington was openly snivelling now, but managed to mutter, "Call my Chaplain, and ask him to find someone suitable."

The Bishop was returned to the cells, and yet again Bryce told the Sergeant to get the prisoner to Westminster in the morning. "But not in the same vehicle as Marlowe. Best to keep those two well apart!"

CHAPTER 24

On the way back to Scotland Yard, Bryce realised that he hadn't told Haig about Hartley, and explained that the peer was coming in later, voluntarily. He also briefed the Inspector on what he had set Kittow and Drummond to do.

"There's a lot of detail in the stuff Barratt sent us, and it'll need a more experienced lawyer than I am to sort through it and see whether it provides a case against Hartley on its own. I think it's more likely that it'll give us a few pointers as to where we could gather more evidence ourselves. Regrettably, the probability of getting a conviction after all this time will be low, so I doubt if we can even charge him.

"Anyway, he's coming at three, armed with his lawyer. I'll meet you at the front desk a few minutes before.

***

Bryce found Kittow among piles of papers, and was pleased to see that the young man was employing a system in his task. The DCS told him to carry on, and went to sit at his desk, where he found an internal envelope addressed to himself. He quickly scanned the contents, smiled, and looked across the room at Kittow.

"A bit of news for you," he started, "I've recommended you for promotion to Detective Sergeant, and I'm pleased to tell you that the recommendation has been approved. I'll get everything fixed, but I think we'll make the appointment effective from Monday."

"That's so unexpected!" said the overjoyed young man, jumping to his feet. "I hoped to make sergeant in a few years – as we discussed in Hunstanton not long ago. But I never thought it would come so quickly. Thank you a dozen times, sir!"

"Don't mention it again. There will be quite a few changes here, as you'll see over the next few weeks. My promotion, and Alex Haig's, was the beginning of the process. Yours is also part of it. Anyway, you carry on, Sergeant! And don't forget to go and get some lunch."

Bryce settled down to read the Barrett papers. He didn't feel particularly hungry, so when Kittow left to visit the canteen he decided to go for a walk in the Embankment Gardens. He and the new DS arrived back in the office at the same time, and each man settled again to his task. They worked in companiable silence for the next hour. Eventually, Bryce sighed audibly, and put down the paper he was holding.

"I'm going to see Lord Hartley," he said to Kittow. "When you've finished your notes, give them to Mrs Pickford to get typed up. I'll see you later."

Bryce and Haig arrived in the foyer simultaneously. Lord Hartley, similarly punctual, came in less than a minute later. He was accompanied by the same solicitor who was representing David Poole. Haig led the way to an interview room.

"I didn't expect to see you again so soon, Mr Randall," said the DCS. "I didn't oppose bail for your other client – did the Magistrate grant it?"

"He did, yes. Thank you for that consideration. I should explain that I see no conflict between Mr Poole's case and this matter, so I agreed to represent Lord Hartley at this stage."

"Understood. But I suggest you don't enlarge your caseload any further by agreeing to represent the man arrested this morning for attempting to blackmail your clients!"

Hartley pounced on this remark. "You've got the dirty dog, then?"

"Yes; we have your Nemesis, and his little ring. He's been charged with conspiracy to demand money with menaces, and will appear in court tomorrow.

"This matter is now in the public domain. I can tell you that the letter writer is related to the woman who was running the Coates

Employment Bureau. She and her daughter have also been charged with conspiracy to commit blackmail.

"Information was picked up by various servants, and passed to the agency. From there, it went to Nemesis.

"Investigations are still ongoing and, client confidentiality notwithstanding, no doubt Mr Randall has told you as much about David Poole as professional ethics allow.

"I can also tell you that Caspar Charrington has been charged with very serious offences, and will appear in the same court as Nemesis tomorrow morning."

"Who is Nemesis? Do I know him?"

"I doubt it. Dr Simon Marlowe, a palaeontologist.

Hartley shook his head, looking perplexed.

"Anyway, enough of this," continued Bryce. "Six people have been charged in this case – seven if you include Galbraith. That only leaves you.

"On the telephone the other day, you told me the name Julian Barratt didn't ring any bells. You lied to me."

Hartley growled under his breath, but didn't speak.

"Before shooting himself, Barratt swore an affidavit before a Commissioner for Oaths. In it, he explained in some detail how you and he engaged in a number of long firm frauds between

1906 and 1912. He also provided evidence.

"That affidavit was sent to the police, presumably just before he died.

"Will you allow your client to make a statement, Mr Randall?"

The solicitor prevaricated. "I'd like to see what the affidavit actually says, before advising my client."

"I'm sure you would. You'll get to see it after your client is charged. At present, we both know that I don't need to show you."

"This is ridiculous!" barked Hartley. "It's an allegation; nothing more. And, as I said to you the other day, it goes back so far that anyone who might have thought they remembered something is probably senile or six feet under by now."

"Such an affidavit doesn't have the same standing as a dying deposition, Chief Superintendent," said Randall. "I'm not sure whether it would even be admissible in criminal proceedings."

"I don't know that either," agreed Bryce, "we're taking counsel's advice on the point. But at the moment it's providing some excellent ideas as to where to look for other, corroborative, evidence.

"I'm not arresting you today, m'lord. We'll see what happens later.

"However, I will tell you something else. Our friend – well, not your friend – Nemesis, has gone further. It seems Barratt's housemaid, who was the informant in that household, saw and made a copy of the affidavit before it was sent to us. That copy was sold – for a hefty sum, incidentally – to Marlowe.

"Gold dust for him, of course, ranking alongside the facts about Poole and Charrington. But, perhaps concerned that Scotland Yard might not think it worthwhile to investigate matters which occurred forty years ago, Marlowe decided to send a transcript to some newspapers. I'm sure their reporters won't be constrained to the same extent that we are. I guess they're well on the trail already – you may have spotted one of them, Mr Randall, in court when Mr Poole was remanded. Whatever we might think of Marlowe, it can't be said that he isn't even-handed in the matter of priming the press, because he's tipped off the papers about Poole and the Bishop too."

Bryce's voice was at its coldest as he continued. "Oh, and I shouldn't bother to seek a mandatory injunction to force me to reveal the content of the affidavit – you won't get one. Nor would you get one to ban a newspaper from publishing the content. You could of course instruct Mr Randall to sue any paper which published anything implying your guilt. But I think they wouldn't even need a public interest defence. They would say they had written the truth.

"Now, please take your client away, Mr Randall."

Hartley looked as if he was about to explode, but the solicitor took him firmly by the arm and led him out.

After they had gone, Haig started to laugh. To an enquiring look from his boss, he explained.

"It was the way you told them to clear off, sir. But you implied that we're investigating with a view to prosecuting Hartley, which contradicts what you said before about a prosecution for the long firm frauds not succeeding after all these years. So there's no prospect of putting him inside.

"Perhaps not, but if the papers publish things his name will be mud everywhere. Not as good as banging him up, but at least it hopefully means he won't have the nerve to show his face in the House of Lords. And most, if not all of the companies he's involved with, will vote him off their boards, rightly thinking that his name among the directors on their letterheaded paper is hardly likely to add lustre to their company."

Haig's sardonic response summed up how both detectives felt about the crooked peer. "My heart really bleeds for him!"

***

On the way back to his desk, Bryce asked Mrs Pickford if she had been given Kittow's transcript to type. The answer was affirmative; it would be ready in half an hour at most.

Bryce occupied himself writing his report until his secretary came in and handed over the completed transcript, together with Kittow's original.

"Excellent, thank you Mrs Pickford. Will you call downstairs, please, and ask Inspector Haig to come up with DC Kittow. DC Drummond too, if he's back in the building."

All three officers arrived a few minutes later.

Bryce explained the position regarding Lord Hartley. "Any comments?" he enquired.

"If he could be prosecuted and was convicted for those three offences, what do you think he would get, sir?" asked Drummond.

"That would probably depend on how much money was lost, and by how many people. Another factor would be whether one or more of the companies went bust and people lost their jobs as a result. But I'd guess at least ten years."

"Just losing his good name doesn't really compare. At least not in my book, sir," said Kittow.

"Mr Haig and I agree. And I assure you that I'll do my best to see that we devote resources into getting the evidence. But we have to be realistic.

"Drummond, what do you have to tell us?"

"I went to the lab and gave them Marlowe's typewriter and the letter. They promised you'd get the result by telephone before noon tomorrow, and written confirmation soon after.

"I took the other four machines to Coates. I left the one from Mrs Wyatt's house on her desk – hope that was okay, sir.

"The two WPCs said they only received two calls on the special line while they were there. They'll let you have their report, but basically both calls were from what sounded like disgruntled maids in posh households. One was reporting on an affair between her employer and a married man, and the other much the same – an affair between her employer and a married lady."

Drummond slid the bureau keys across the table towards the DCS. He hesitated, and felt his face going red. "Just one other thing, sir. When I first went to the bureau I spoke to a very nice girl in the office there – Miss Berryman. You probably saw her yourself during the raid." He coughed and spluttered, aware that three pairs of eyes were fixed on him. "We, er, we seemed to like each other. Well, I wasn't very happy about having to give her a false name and all that. But when I went back today and explained everything, she didn't hold it against me. Even though I had to throw her and her colleague out and lock the place up, she agreed to come to the pictures with me on Saturday, sir. I hope that's all right?"

Bryce looked penetratingly at the

stammering detective. Turning to Haig, he asked, "Alex, can you think of any precedent in our ranks where an investigating officer furthered his amorous interests with a possible suspect, in the way that Gerry evidently has?"

Drummond, completely missing the cue that the DCS had let the conversation drift into 'informal mode', turned exceedingly anxious eyes to his Inspector.

Haig tried but failed to keep a grin from his face. "Actually, guv, one precedent does come to mind. And that turned out well, as I'm sure you'll agree!"

Bryce laughed. "Not fair of me to tease you, Drummond. The Inspector will explain later why we're amused. And yes, I did notice your young lady – she looked a nice bright girl."

Haig nodded in agreement. Kittow, sitting beside Drummond, playfully punched him on the shoulder and grinned at his colleague's evident embarrassment, although he wasn't aware of the 'precedent' either.

"Certainly it's all right," continued the DCS, "nothing whatever to do with me. Would have been quite different if she'd been involved in the blackmail, of course."

"Well done. While you were arranging to meet pretty girls at Coates, Kittow has been busy converting the critical information in the files, and in the accounts book, into a simple easy-to-read list.

"Potentially, we could have a number of other people who are guilty of serious offences. As police officers, we should investigate material coming our way which suggests that. However, glancing at the numbers here, that looks like a huge task, and I'm in two minds about it.

"So I think we'll only look at instances where the victim either paid a large sum of money, say over £250, or repeatedly paid smaller sums of money. That implies a fairly serious matter – which still might not be criminal, of course, in which case it's not police business and we go no further.

"One last thing. This case has gone very well, and the AC has already recognised the fact. Although there's still a lot of work to do, we've broken the back of it remarkably quickly. I'm very pleased with all of you.

"Drummond, you haven't worked with me on an 'away' case like these two, but you may have heard that we have enjoyable meals on those occasions. Or," he added, noticing Haig's expression, "perhaps it would be more accurate to say that we enjoy the company even though the food itself hasn't always been too marvellous.

"I don't want to set a precedent for Met cases, but I'd like to take you all out for a meal tomorrow evening. I thought a fish-and-chip supper at that restaurant in Seven Dials would be a good idea. I've been a couple of times and really enjoyed it. No problem with rationing, either. My favourite food, really."

Three very happy policemen gratefully accepted the invitation and left the Chief Superintendent's office, having agreed that, unless some unforeseen matter arose, they would meet in Endell Street at seven o'clock the next evening.

CHAPTER 25

Friday 10th November, 1950

Just before nine o'clock the following morning, the DCS put in a call to a set of chambers in Holborn, and asked for Angela Lacon. He spoke first to her clerk, but as soon as he identified himself he was put through to her room.

Bryce was an old friend, having known the barrister and her husband since before the war, when all three were reading for the bar. He was also an honorary uncle to their two children. A few minutes were spent in pleasantries.

"Are you in Court this morning?" he asked.

"No, for a change. Quite an idle day ahead, actually. Preparation for a case up in Liverpool next week. What is it you need, Philip? I can certainly make time to see you if you want to come along."

"Thanks, Angie. I just want you to look through some papers and advise me. You can bill the Yard for it, of course. Will ten-thirty suit you?"

Bryce put down the telephone, and for

the third consecutive morning, left the building and walked along to the nearby Magistrates' Court. He handed various papers to the Inspector who was prosecuting in the remand court, and explained various points which might be queried.

"I have no idea who is representing the Bishop. I gather Marlowe will employ the same solicitor as the Wyatts' yesterday – did he ask for bail for them, by the way?"

"He did, sir, but it was refused," replied the prosecutor.

"Good. Object even more strenuously when it comes to Marlowe and the Bishop – although I can't see any beak granting bail to those two sub-humans."

Leaving the court, he hopped on a bus which took him as far as Oxford Circus, where he took a Central Line train to Chancery Lane. A short walk up Gray's Inn Road brought him to his destination.

Miss Lacon's clerk had met him before, and after a quick chat suggested he go straight up. "I'll bring you coffee and so on shortly, sir."

In the barrister's room the two friends exchanged a hug, and Angela waved him to a chair.

"Before I get down to why I'm here, Angie, I'd like to tell you that Vee is expecting a baby – due around April next year."

"Oh, that's wonderful, Philip," cried his

friend, coming round the desk and hugging him again. "Only snag is that I guess my two will see even less of you. But pass on our congratulations to Veronica. Such happy news!"

Bryce drew a folder from his briefcase. Giving a short summary of the background, he explained that he wanted an opinion regarding the prospects of a successful prosecution on the long firm fraud cases – particularly on the admissibility of the affidavit and other material Barratt had sent to the police, and what additional evidence it would be essential to obtain.

"Hartley, eh," said Angela. "I've never spoken to him, although we've been in the same room a few times.

"I assume you don't expect me to speak off the top of my head, so I'll read this lot this afternoon, and give you a call later. I'll let you have a written opinion by Monday."

One of the assistant clerks arrived with coffee. When he had gone Bryce continued.

"There are some even more juicy ones," said Bryce. "I've charged five other people in this case already. Ask around to see what's available. There's David Poole MP; conspiracy to pervert the course of justice. The Bishop of Crewe; serious offences against children. Plus three large-scale blackmailers who, incidentally, provided the information on Hartley and the other two."

"Some case, Philip! A pity it's unethical to

tout for briefs!"

The two sat chatting until they finished their coffee, when Bryce stood up to go.

"I'll call Veronica in the next day or so," said Angela, "and get you two round for dinner. Also, my father-in-law keeps pestering us to bring you two to stay again. I swear he thinks more of you than he does of us! Anyway, I'll get Vee to put a weekend in your diary."

***

Back at the Yard, Bryce found a message from the police laboratory.

'Latest typewriter undoubtedly the one used to write your letters. Paper also identical. Written report follows.'

Bryce wandered happily downstairs to see how his men were doing. The three detectives had commandeered a small meeting room. In this they had set up an easel, on which was a cork board with various bits of paper pinned to it.

"Good news from the lab, reported the DCS. "Marlowe's typewriter is the one used by Nemesis. How's it going in here?"

"Pretty well, sir," replied Haig. "We've identified the probable informant in the Bishop's palace, and the one in Poole's household. We've also located Fletcher's valet, Roberts. It's a question now of contacting them. We could do that for all three via their employers' telephones, but before doing that I wanted to see if you thought it better to drop in on them without warning – otherwise they might scarper."

Bryce considered this for a moment.

"I don't think they'll run, but as we need statements, someone must go and see them anyway. There's no desperate hurry, so no point in making telephone contact.

"Incidentally, I'm not concerned about protecting these people. When their employers – whoever they may be now – find out what's been going on, I'd expect each servant to be discharged anyway.

"Kittow, when you've finished going through these lists, you can have the job of visiting the key servants and getting statements. Take Drummond with you."

The DCS left his men to their tasks, and returned to his office and his own workload, glad to have no appointments and some uninterrupted 'desk time'.

CHAPTER 26

In Seven Dials, the four policemen rendezvoused at the famous fish-and-chip restaurant, arriving outside almost simultaneously.

The establishment didn't attempt the pretence of a *maitre d' hotel*, but Bryce gave his name to a waitress, who led them upstairs and across the room to a well-placed table.

"I'll come back in a couple of minutes for your orders," she told the seated detectives. "Any drinks first?"

All four asked for bitter. When the girl returned with a tray holding pint glasses, the food orders given to her were also identical – cod, chips, and mushy peas.

"Cheers," said Bryce, raising his glass to his men. "And thank you all for your work on this case."

"Cheers," responded his team in unison.

When everyone had taken a good swallow of ale, Bryce continued. "Gerry and I went for lunch in The Albert recently, and I explained my rules for informality – which I suppose is a contradiction in terms, really. Other officers don't operate to the same rules. You may not know this, but the AC(C) calls me 'Philip' even on duty. But I can't see myself calling him 'Patrick', even if we were both guests at the same party."

The others readily understood their boss's reticence. Drummond had never even seen the man, but Haig and Kittow couldn't visualise anyone below the Chief Commissioner daring to address Mr Anderson-Hall as 'Patrick' either.

"Changing the subject, guv, while Adam and I were waiting for Fletcher to get home, we talked about the railway lines in Kent and Sussex. I was trying to educate him about the early companies, but it was an uphill battle."

Kittow laughed. "I have to admit it's very impressive that someone from Scotland is so knowledgeable about the south east. I was born in Kent, and I didn't know a tenth of what Alex has already told me about the county."

"Ah, but just hear the guv, Adam – he knows a sight more than I do. Ask him some time about how the London terminus stations for the Kent and Sussex trains came to be built where they are."

Bryce gave a self-deprecating grin. "I can't deny that this is one of my favourite topics."

Drummond, who hadn't spoken so far, thought it was a good idea to mention the test which he had been set.

"Ah, yes, Gerry," said Kittow, "on a recent

case, I learned a lot about Edwin Lutyens. Very interesting it was too, I have to admit."

Bryce grinned. "When I was trying to interest Gerry in the Piccadilly Line extension, I may have possibly mentioned Lutyens in passing. We all have our heroes!"

"Oh, and you haven't been singled out for this treatment, Gerry," added Kittow. "He gave me a test very similar to yours!"

"Don't tell him about it now, Adam – it might give him ideas," laughed the DCS.

"Now, this is work-related, but we remain informal. I'm not sure if Adam has told you about his imminent promotion, but if not I can tell you that from Monday he is to be DS. Adam, I think you should know is that Alex here also recommended you – as it happens he was too late, because the matter was already in hand, but still.

Kittow raised a hand in salute to Haig. "That's much appreciated, Alex. I've already thanked the guv, of course. I can still hardly believe it."

"I'm just the same," said Haig.

Bryce continued. "So that's three of us with a move upwards, and in part this meal is to celebrate that.

"Don't feel out of it, Gerry. Alex and Adam both spent several years as detective constables, and as uniformed constables before that – your turn will undoubtedly come. That's if you pass the Piccadilly Line station test, of course! Perhaps Miss Berryman will go with you to do that, and act as a second pair of eyes."

Haig and Kittow laughed, and Drummond – who had already thought about inviting Anna to accompany him – blushed, silently hoping she would agree.

"Well, gentlemen," said Bryce, "this is the beginning of what's really a new era at the Yard – and you are all going to play crucial parts in it.

"I have just one more snippet of information for you before we switch off from all work matters. I had a call back from Treasury Counsel – two of you have met Angela Lacon. She says there's enough to charge Hartley, and thinks that we should be able to obtain a couple more bits of evidence which would be enough to secure a conviction.

"Cheers again!" he said, just as the plates of food arrived.

****

AFTERWORD

AUTHOR'S NOTES ON

SECTION 29 OF THE 1916 LARCENY ACT

The wording of this Act of Parliament, like most legislation of its time, is somewhat arcane – and some of the content certainly wouldn't fit with 21st century mores.

In summary, Section 29 deals with blackmail – even though that word doesn't appear anywhere in the statute.

For the purposes of this book, there are perhaps two key points:

i) Although blackmail is often referred to as 'demanding money with menaces', it doesn't have to involve money. The demand can be for 'any property or valuable thing'.

ii) The 'menaces' don't necessarily have to involve threats of physical violence; accusing or threatening to accuse someone of a serious crime is sufficient.

Just before this story is set, the 1948

Criminal Justice Act abolished penal servitude ('hard labour'), and substituted the same period of ordinary imprisonment. Judicial corporal punishment (which was available under S29 in certain circumstances), and the right of a peer to be tried by the House of Lords (relevant to this story), were both abolished at the same time.

S29 remained in force until the 1968 Theft Act – which **does** use the term 'blackmail', and condenses the legislation into three very short paragraphs. The maximum sentence today is fourteen years rather than 'life'.

The current Act also covers another point raised in the book. It now states:

"...if with a view to gain for himself or another **or with intent to cause loss to another**..."

BOOKS IN THIS SERIES

Chief Inspector Bryce Mysteries
A series of stories about a Scotland Yard detective in the late 1940s and early 1950s.

The Bedroom Window Murder

It is 1949. Sir Francis Sherwood – WW1 hero, landowner, magistrate – is shot dead while standing at an open bedroom window in his country house. A rifle is found in the grounds.

The county police seek help from Scotland Yard.

Detective Chief Inspector Bryce and Detective Sergeant Haig are assigned to the case. The first difficulty for the Yard men is that nobody with even a mild dislike of Sherwood can be found.

But before that problem can be resolved, others arise...

The Courthouse Murder

In July 1949, an unpopular and deeply unpleasant man is stabbed in the courthouse of an English city. As the murder has been committed in a room to which the general public doesn't have access, it seems probable that the culprit is someone involved with the business of the courts.

Suspects include a number of lawyers, police officers, and magistrates.

For various reasons, the local Chief Constable decides to ask Scotland Yard to investigate the murder.

Chief Inspector Philip Bryce and Sergeant Alex Haig are assigned to the case.

Theirs is a recent partnership, but the two men worked well together in another murder case a few weeks before. (See 'The Bedroom Window Murder'.)

The Felixstowe Murder

In August 1949, Detective Chief Inspector Bryce and his new bride are holidaying in the East Anglian seaside resort of Felixstowe.

During afternoon tea in the Palm Court of their hotel, a man dies at a nearby table.

Reluctant to get directly involved, Bryce nevertheless agrees to help the inexperienced local police inspector get to grips with his first murder case, turning his own honeymoon into a 'busman's holiday'.

Multiples Of Murder

Three more cases for Philip Bryce. The first two are set in 1949, and follow on from The Bedroom Window Murder, The Courthouse Murder, and The Felixstowe Murder.
The third goes back to 1946, when Bryce – not long back in the police after his army service – was a mere Detective Inspector, based in Whitechapel rather than Scotland Yard.

1. In the office kitchen of a small advertising agency in London, a man falls to the floor, dead. Initially, it is believed that he had some sort of heart attack, but it soon becomes clear that he had received a fatal electric shock. A faulty kettle is then blamed. But evidence emerges showing that this was not an accident. Chief Inspector Bryce is assigned to the case.

2. Just before opening time, a body is found in

the larger pool at the huge public baths in St Marylebone. The man has been shot, presumably the previous evening. It is DCI Bryce's task, aided by Detective Sergeant Haig and others, to discover the identity of the victim, why he was killed, and who shot him.

3. For a few months in 1946, a traditional London bus was modified in an experiment to allow passengers to 'Pay-As-You-Board'. Doors were fitted, instead of having the usual open platform. The stairs rose from inside the saloon rather than directly from the platform. On the upper deck, a man is found stabbed to death. None of the passengers can shed any light on the murder, yet the design of this bus meant that no-one could have jumped off the bus unnoticed – one of them must be the murderer. Inspector Bryce, together with colleagues from Leman Street police station, solves one of his earlier cases.

Death At Mistram Manor

In September 1949, a wake is being held at a manor house in Oxfordshire, following the burial of the chatelaine. Over a hundred mourners are present.

Within an hour, the clergyman who conducted

the funeral service is taken ill himself. The local doctor, present at the wake, provisionally diagnoses appendicitis, and calls for an ambulance. However, the priest dies soon after being admitted to hospital.

An autopsy reveals that the cause of death was strychnine poisoning.

The circumstances are such that accidental ingestion and suicide are both ruled out. The rector was murdered, and the timing means that the poison must have been taken during the wake.

The local police, faced with a lengthy list of potential suspects, ask Scotland Yard to take on the investigation, and the case is assigned to Detective Chief Inspector Bryce and two colleagues.

Although most of the mourners can easily be eliminated from the enquiry, around eight of them cannot. The experienced London officers have to sift through a number of initially-promising indications, before finally being able to identify the killer.

Machinations Of A Murderer

There are at least two reasons why Robin

Whitaker wants to eliminate his wife, Dulcie. He is not allowed to drink any alcohol, nor to gamble.

Dulcie controls his life to an extent that he finds intolerable. But she is also wealthy, so merely leaving her is not an acceptable option.

In most circumstances Dr Whitaker thinks and acts like the very intelligent and highly-educated man he is. However, he has somehow convinced himself that the action of killing his wife is justified. He is also certain that his innate brainpower will give him a significant edge over any police detectives, and allow him to outwit them with ease.

What are his thoughts? How does he make his decisions? What does he do?

Will he get away with murder?

Suspicions Of A Parlourmaid; The Norfolk Railway Murders

Two more cases for Philip Bryce.

1 An affluent elderly lady dies. The death certificate cites 'natural causes', but the servants are uncomfortable.

A parlourmaid decides to go to New Scotland Yard, and talk to someone there. She is fortunate, because Detective Sergeant Haig happens to pass through the foyer while she is explaining. The busy desk officer intercepts him, and asks to him to listen to the maid's story.

Haig listens politely, but is ready to dismiss the story as tittle-tattle, when he hears one thing which makes him take notice. He goes to report to his boss, DCI Bryce, who also finds the point of interest, and speaks to the maid himself.

The full might of the Metropolitan Police is then focused on the matter – and a post mortem examination reveals that the lady certainly did not die from natural causes.

In the leafy South London suburb of Dulwich Village, Bryce and Haig investigate the happenings, and sort out who is innocent, and who is guilty.

2. DCI Bryce is sent to Norfolk, where two solicitors have been killed. There are obvious connections between the crimes. First, both men were partners in the same firm. But also, both appeared to have been killed while travelling on local railway trains, and the bodies then thrown out. Over the whole existence of railways in Britain, the number of such cases could be

counted on the fingers of one hand. So one such case would have been rare enough, but for there to be two – on different trains and a few days apart – was almost unbelievable.

However, shortly before these two men were found, a third body was discovered. This victim didn't seem to have any connection to the firm of solicitors – but he too was found beside a railway track.

A temporary absence of CID officers in King's Lynn causes the Chief Constable to ask Scotland Yard to take the case. DCI Bryce and two of his officers travel to West Norfolk, where they find a local Detective Constable eager to help.

Which of the three victims was the real target, and which murders were either dry runs or red herrings?

This Village Is Cursed

A young provincial journalist receives a telephone call from a man who won't give his name. Anticipating the scoop of his career, Marcus Cunningham arranges to meet the informant at Liverpool Street station.

Subsequent events quickly draw in Scotland Yard

detectives Chief Inspector Philip Bryce and his colleague Sergeant Alex Haig, as they conduct a complex murder investigation.

The Amateur Detective

In 1950, a death occurs under the uniquely-banded cliffs in Hunstanton. It is soon realised that this is a case of murder, but the Norfolk police inspector runs into difficulties, and Scotland Yard DCI Philip Bryce finds himself back in the county for the second time in a matter of months.

A local amateur detective with a considerable knowledge of murder cases (both real and fictional) is determined to help the police, and comes up with various suggestions. However, initially neither he nor the police seem to be able to pin all the usual key elements – means, motive, and opportunity – on any one person.

With the possible list of suspects narrowed down to relations of the deceased and a group of bridge-playing friends, will the amateur measure up to the standards of sleuthing shown by his fictional heroes, and solve the case ahead of the professionals?

Eventually, one person ends up in the dock at the Assizes in Norwich – but the drama still hasn't ended!